# MEGAN'S
# ISLAND

Aladdin Paperbacks by Willo Davis Roberts

Don't Hurt Laurie!
Megan's Island
The Minden Curse
The Pet-Sitting Peril
Sugar Isn't Everything
The View from the Cherry Tree

# MEGAN'S ISLAND

## Willo Davis Roberts

Aladdin Paperbacks

Aladdin Paperbacks
An imprint of Simon & Schuster
Children's Publishing Division
1230 Avenue of the Americas
New York, NY 10020

First Aladdin Paperbacks edition 1990

A hardcover edition of *Megan's Island* is available from Atheneum Books for Young Readers.

Printed in the United States of America


Library of Congress Cataloging-in-Publication Data
Roberts, Willo Davis.
    Megan's island / Willow Davis Roberts. — 1st Aladdin ed.
        p.    cm.
    Originally published: New York : Atheneum, 1988.
    Summary: First eleven-year-old Megan is astonished when her mother insists on taking her and her younger brother up to the lake cottage a week before school is out; then they find mysterious strangers following them.
    ISBN 0-689-83867-0
    [1. Single-parent family—Fiction.   2. Mystery and detective stories.]
I. Title.
PZ7.R54465Me      1990
[Fic]—dc20                                                89-18457

*To*
**MATTHEW**
*who loves books*

## one

THERE WAS one week of school left on the day the peculiar things began to happen.

At first Megan didn't realize there was anything wrong. She was thinking about the terrific summer that stretched ahead of her, most of it to be spent with her best friend, Annie. They'd made all kinds of plans.

"We'll go to the pool every day, and skating at the rink," Annie had mused.

"And sit in the backyard and talk," Megan added. "And eat apples and peanut-butter-and-jelly sandwiches." Annie *loved* peanut-butter-and-jelly sandwiches. "And when Mom takes her vacation in July, maybe your folks will let you go with us to the lake where Grandpa Davis is staying until his foot heals so he can go back to work."

Annie had sighed in delight. "It sounds fantastic," she murmured.

"There's a lovely private beach," Karen Collier had told the girls, "and you can fish with my dad, or lie around doing nothing—whatever you like—for two whole weeks."

Neither Megan nor her brother, Sandy, had ever been swimming anywhere outside of a pool, except for once when they'd had a picnic on the shore of Lake Michigan. The lake where Grandpa had the cottage wasn't nearly as big as Lake Michigan, but that meant the water would be warmer. And unlike many of the lakes in northern Minnesota, this one had a sandy beach instead of a mucky bottom, so it would be *almost* as nice as the big lake.

The whole idea made Megan happy just to think about it. Megan and Annie had discussed it in a whisper in school that day. Both were hoping their parents would buy them new swimsuits before July. And Mr. Boldt had said, "Vacation's not for another week, girls. Let's keep our minds on reviewing math for another day or two, all right?"

Annie had blushed, but Megan knew Mr. Boldt wasn't really annoyed with them. He was looking forward to vacation, too. He'd already told them he was spending his summer on Prince Edward Island, up in Canada, and he'd promised to bring back pictures of the red cliffs and beaches, and of the house where Anne in *Anne of Green Gables* had lived. (Well, really it was the author of the book who had lived there, but Mr. Boldt said it was almost the same thing.)

Annie had always gone to Fairview School, and she took it for granted. Megan, however, had been there just this year, in the sixth grade. Before that, her family had moved quite a bit. Her mother said it was hard for a woman alone to find a job that paid enough to let her support two kids.

Once in a while, Megan thought about how nice it would be to have two parents—maybe even a mother who could stay home instead of having to go to work every day—so that money wouldn't be such a problem. She knew that if Grandpa Davis hadn't sent a check every month or two, making ends meet would have been much more difficult for the Collier family. Her mother's salary just about covered the rent and the grocery bill, with almost never anything left over.

"Megan! Come set the table, please!" her mother called that evening.

"Coming," Megan responded, reluctantly closing her book and sliding off the bed. Her mind was still on the story, the adventures of a girl and her father in the wilderness. She wondered if she would have had adventures of that kind, too, if her father hadn't died when she was a baby. Well, when Sandy was a baby, really, she amended. Megan herself had been three when it happened, though she didn't remember it.

Annie's dad didn't take her camping, but he sometimes gave her the money to treat Megan to a movie or an afternoon of skating. Megan was sure her own dad had been like Annie's, friendly and generous. She sighed, walking into the kitchen and opening the cupboard to get out the dishes.

"Mom, did Daddy like camping and things like that?" she asked.

For a moment the knife Mrs. Collier was using to chop vegetables stopped making sounds against the wooden board. When Megan turned, the plates held in both hands, her mother's face had taken on that stillness she usually got when the subject of her husband came up.

Because she could tell that it still hurt to talk about him, even after all these years, Megan didn't often mention her father. She'd been thinking about the book she was reading, and this time she'd spoken without considering her mother's feelings.

Mrs. Collier began to chop again, and her face smoothed out. "No, I'm afraid not, honey. He wasn't an outdoorsman, not the way Grandpa Davis is. Hand me that bowl, will you?"

For some reason Megan persisted. Maybe it was because, for just this minute, she wished so hard that she had a father.

"What *did* he like to do?"

Again the chopping blade hesitated, though only momentarily. "Oh, dancing. He was a good dancer."

"And reading?"

"No. He wasn't much of a reader, either."

"What, then? He must have done something besides dance."

"He liked sports," her mother said after a moment, reaching for a tomato to slice. "He went to ball games, fights, things like that. Megan, maybe you'd better call Sandy. The casserole will be out of the oven in a few minutes."

Tuna casserole again. She could tell by the smell. Megan sighed. Tuna casserole was becoming her least favorite food, but it was cheap. She wondered if she dared broach the subject of a new swimsuit tonight, or if she should wait until the next time they got a check from Grandpa, which usually put her mother in a good mood.

Sandy had been playing kick-the-can, and he was hot and sweaty. Sandy was ten, a year younger than Megan, and everyone always knew they were brother and sister. They were both slim and had blue eyes and reddish-gold hair that curled. Well, Megan's only waved, though her mother said if she'd cut it short it would curl like Sandy's. Megan didn't want to cut it. It reached halfway down her back, and it was the prettiest thing about her. She knew her face was perfectly ordinary, but everybody said she had beautiful hair. When they noticed that, they forgave her the sprinkling of freckles across her nose.

As Sandy headed for the table, their mother made good-natured scolding noises. "Wash first, please!"

He sniffed at the dish she was removing from the oven. "Tuna casserole again? I don't know if it's worth washing for."

"Then don't eat," Mrs. Collier said calmly. "We're economizing tonight so that on Sunday we can have baked ham. If you want to wait until then to wash in order to eat, it's all right with me."

"I wish it were Sunday now," Sandy commented as he disappeared in the direction of the bathroom.

Megan plucked a slice of cucumber out of the salad bowl. It reminded her of the green bathing suit she'd seen at K-Mart. She'd better not wait until Grandpa sent a check to lay the groundwork, not if she didn't want the money spent before Mom set aside enough for the suit.

"Annie and I were looking at the swimsuits they have on sale at the mall," she began.

Mrs. Collier sighed. "On sale already, and it's only the first week in June? Too bad for anyone who needs a new suit in August. By then they'll be selling snowsuits, I suppose. You forgot the napkins, honey."

Megan absentmindedly reached for the plastic container holding the paper napkins. "I saw this one, it was pale green, and in my size. My old one's getting awfully short, Mom. I've let the straps out as far as I can. I'll be needing a suit all summer, for here and if we go to the lake. Annie's getting one—red with a white stripe across here. . . ."

It wasn't quite true. Annie's mother hadn't yet agreed to the new suit, but she probably would. Annie's dad was a bank manager, and at their house it wasn't a question of whether or not they could afford it. The Van Dows never actually had to go without anything important.

"Oh, Megan . . ." Her mother stared at her helplessly, then shrugged. "Well, maybe, when Grandpa sends another check—but I don't know if he'll be able to for the rest of the summer, honey. He's up at the lake, you know, because he hurt his foot. Until he goes back to work he probably won't have much money to spare."

Megan hadn't thought about that. Disappointment coursed through her, and she didn't pursue the matter. She knew it made her mother feel bad when she couldn't do things for them. Megan ate her tuna casserole with a lump in her throat.

After she'd cleared the table, Megan took the trash out to the can near the alley. She was on the back steps, returning to the kitchen, where Sandy was washing the dishes and her mother was putting them away, when she heard the crash.

Megan pulled open the screen door and stared at broken fragments of glass all over the floor. Her mother, who had changed into shorts when she came home from work, was looking down at her bare feet amidst the shards of what had been her favorite salad bowl.

"Hey, you cut your feet!" Sandy exclaimed. "You OK, Mom?"

Mrs. Collier reached over and turned off the little portable TV they often carried into the kitchen to entertain them while they did dull chores there. "Yes, I guess so. Megan, get the broom and sweep this up before I try to walk, will you? Sandy, would you bring the first-aid kit?"

It wasn't until they'd cleaned out the small cuts, and put a Band-Aid over the worst one, that Megan asked, "What happened, anyway?"

"The bowl just slipped out of my hands, I guess. Clumsy me," Mrs. Collier said.

She wasn't usually clumsy. She never tripped over her own feet, as Megan and Sandy often did.

"I'm sorry about the bowl. Grandma gave it to you the year before she died, didn't she?"

"Yes. Here, Sandy, you can put this back in the bathroom." Mrs. Collier passed over the first-aid kit and stood up, putting out a hand to a chair back to steady herself.

"You look pale, Mom," Megan said, and her mother shook her head.

"Silly. It was such a little bit of blood," she said. "Finish putting the dishes away for me before you go to Annie's, will you?"

She left Megan alone in the kitchen, wondering. Her mother had never gotten pale or faint at the sight of blood before. When Sandy had cut his hand so badly it required twelve stitches, their mother hadn't turned a hair. It was puzzling.

Two hours later, when she came back from Annie's, where they'd played tetherball in the backyard, Megan found her mother doing something even more puzzling.

She was in Megan's room, putting clothes into a big suitcase.

"Mom? What's going on?" Megan watched her mother hastily fold a pair of pink shorts and a green-and-white-striped shirt together, as if they matched.

"We're leaving for the lake tonight," Mrs. Collier said. "Finish this, will you? I've cleaned out the two top drawers. Do the rest of those, and then get the stuff out of the closet. Just pack what you'll need at the lake; put everything else into those boxes. I've asked Jenny to see to our things, put everything in storage."

Shock made Megan's mouth dry. "Tonight? Mom, there's still a week of school!"

"Missing the last few days won't hurt either of you. You've already had your tests, haven't you? It's just parties and busywork, you said so yourself. Don't forget to take a couple of sweaters—early mornings on the water can be chilly."

"Mom! Why? How come we're going? And why tonight? It's a long way to the lake, and it's almost nine o'clock now. . . ."

Her mother grew very still, so that apprehension crept over Megan and made her still, too.

"Honey, please do as I say and don't ask any questions now. I don't have time to answer them. I've never asked you to do anything unreasonable, have I? Well, trust me now. I'll explain when I can. All right?"

Her mother's attempt at a smile was pathetic. Megan's throat closed, and she couldn't answer.

When her mother crossed the hall and began to give Sandy the same instructions, Megan scarcely heard her younger brother's startled protest.

It didn't make sense. Even though they'd moved around a lot, they'd never skipped the last week of school before. And Annie was supposed to go with them to the lake, after school was out. Mrs. Van Dow would never allow

Annie to skip the last week of school and go with them now.

Megan stepped to the doorway. Her voice wavered. "Mom, what about . . ."

"Not now, Megan. Please, just pack your things right away."

Megan felt tears prickling in her eyes. Something was wrong. Terribly wrong.

# two

"MEGAN?"

She turned at the whisper to find Sandy in the doorway. They could hear their mother in her own room as he came toward Megan, staring down at the suitcase she had just closed.

"What's going on?" he wanted to know.

"Your guess is as good as mine. You were home all evening. Did Mom get a phone call or something?"

Sandy shook his head. "I never heard it ring."

"Or something in the mail that upset her?"

"Nothing but a catalog. Are we really going to Grandpa's without finishing school?"

"It sure sounds like it," Megan said. "She seemed OK before supper. Then she broke her best salad bowl and cut her feet a little bit, and I went over to Annie's. When I got back she said we were going to leave tonight for the lake, and not to ask questions now. What did she do while I was gone?"

Sandy sank onto the edge of the bed. "She went in her bedroom and closed the door. She took the telephone with her, so she must have called somebody."

"Jenny." Jenny Halloway was Mrs. Collier's best friend at the office where they both worked. "She said she'd asked Jenny to put our things in storage."

She watched her brother's face as that sifted through his mind. "You mean we're not going for just a couple of weeks? We're not coming back here? Ever?"

The fear was stronger now. "I don't know. If the stuff's in storage I guess . . ." Her voice trailed off. She didn't know what it meant. "It was funny, her breaking the bowl that way. She never breaks things."

"Not like me," Sandy said, nodding.

"I thought she'd be upset about it. It was the last thing Grandma gave her. But except for telling me to sweep up the glass, she didn't even seem to think about the bowl. What happened to make her drop it?"

"I don't know. I was washing dishes, and she was drying things and putting them in the cupboard. In between, she was watching TV, I guess."

"What was on?" Megan asked.

"The news, I think. Or maybe it was nearly time for it. I wasn't paying any attention. I was thinking about the ball game tomorrow. I'm not going to get to play now, am I?"

They both jumped when Mrs. Collier spoke from the doorway. "Finished? I'm going to back the car out. Put the suitcases in the trunk, Sandy. We'll be ready to go in a few minutes."

For a moment after she turned away, they were speechless. "We're really going to go. At ten o'clock at night," Sandy said, incredulous.

Megan took a few steps after her mother. "Mom, I've got to call Annie. I can't just leave. . . ."

"No. No, don't call anyone. You can get in touch with Annie later. It's too late tonight," her mother said firmly.

"Well, Annie will be asleep, but her folks always watch the late news—I can just explain to them. . . ." Explain what? she wondered. That her mother had apparently lost her mind?

"No. No phone calls." To emphasize that, Mrs. Collier stooped and unplugged the telephone from the wall and wound the cord around it on the table where it stood. "Come on, kids, load the car. It's going to take all night to get there, and I want to make it by dawn if we can."

"Mom . . ." Megan said, pleading, and not only for permission to make the call to Annie. She was scared, and she needed to know what was happening.

She got a hug, but it didn't help. "I know I'm upsetting you. Believe me, it's necessary that we go right away. I'll tell you why when I can. Here, you take that bag, Sandy— Megan and I will get the rest."

There was nothing to do but obey, though Megan's mind whirled. No finishing school. No last-day picnic. No summer with Annie. What would Annie think when Megan didn't show up to walk to school tomorrow? When she called and there was no answer? When she rang the bell and learned the house was empty? When, after she'd been invited to go with Megan to the lake for a vacation, the whole Collier family just disappeared?

Did Jenny know why they were leaving? If Megan called Jenny right now and asked, would she learn anything?

No, she decided. She probably didn't have time before her mother came back, and even if she did, grownups always stuck together. Jenny wouldn't tell her what was going on. She'd say, "Ask your mother."

The big suitcase was so heavy it took both hands to haul it off the bed. Megan staggered down the hallway with it, and stumbled over a wastebasket near the front door, overturning it. She stopped in disgust to pick up the spilled contents.

The last thing she picked up didn't immediately go back into the wastebasket. She swallowed, looking at it, jumping guiltily when Sandy came back inside for another load.

"What's the matter?" he demanded.

"Nothing," Megan lied, and dropped the torn envelope in with the other trash. The envelope was addressed to Mrs. Lightner, their landlady, and was torn nearly in half, so that the check inside showed through the tear.

Why was her mother tearing up the rent check she'd intended to mail tomorrow?

The only reason Megan could think of was that they weren't going to live here anymore. They weren't going to pay the rent for the coming month. Whatever was the matter was serious, and they weren't coming back.

The fear inside Megan grew until she felt suffocated with it, unable to breathe. Yet there was nothing she could do except go with Sandy and their mother.

MRS. COLLIER turned on the car radio to a program of soft music as they sped through the night. Occasionally they went through a town where there were lights around them for a few minutes. Mostly they were on the open highway with only an occasional set of oncoming headlights to break the darkness, or the diminishing red sparks of taillights as a car passed them at high speed.

In the back seat, solidly surrounded by bundles and boxes, blankets and pillows, Sandy slept. Megan was tired, too, but for some time she couldn't follow her brother's example.

She rested her head on the back of the seat, wishing she dared to press her mother for the answers she was almost afraid to hear. What could have sent them into flight this way, without even telling Annie she was going?

It *was* flight, Megan thought. They were running from something, but what? She couldn't imagine anything that could have caused her mother to be scared enough to run away.

She turned her head slightly, intending to ask if there weren't time, finally, to explain. Her mother's profile showed in the dim light from the dashboard, and something about it made the question die in Megan's throat, unspoken.

She had seen her mother tired, and cross, and nearly sick with worry, but usually the anxiety was over how to pay for something important. Megan had never seen her looking this way.

Her mother, too, was afraid.

Her heart beating a nervous tattoo in her chest, Megan willed herself to be calm. To wait, until her mother was ready to talk.

When they got to Grandpa's, she thought. Then her mother would tell her what was going on.

After a while, she slept.

She woke as the sky was growing pink and gray in the

east. Her mouth was dry, and there was a crick in her neck because her head had rolled sideways.

Her mother glanced at her as she stretched and groaned. "Good morning. I hope you got a good rest."

Her mother had had no rest. She had driven all night, with only one stop to get gas and use a restroom.

"I was dreaming," Megan said, aware that she was hungry. Normally she would have had a snack before she went to bed last night, but the turn of events had driven hunger right out of her mind. "About Daddy, when I was a little girl, and he tossed me in the air and laughed."

Mrs. Collier turned on her flasher and swung the car out around a slow-moving truck. "Do you remember him, Megan?"

"No, not really. He had red hair, though, didn't he? Like Sandy's and mine? And he was strong and good looking."

"Yes."

"I knew he was my dad, in the dream. I wish he hadn't died." Maybe, if he were still with them, they wouldn't be running this way. He would be taking care of whatever the problem was. Daddies weren't afraid of things the way kids and mothers sometimes were. Or were they? Until last night, she hadn't thought mothers got scared, either— not scared enough to drive away from home in the middle of the night without telling anyone.

Her mother didn't answer, concentrating on her driving. "It's only a few more miles now."

"Does Grandpa know we're coming?"

Mrs. Collier shook her head. "No phone, remember?"

So they hadn't set this up between them ahead of time, through their usual letters. If they had, she'd have told the children before last night. That only made it more peculiar than it already was.

The village sign said *Welcome to Lakewood, Minnesota— Population 840—A Friendly Town;* a big, fancy sign for such a small place. And then they were slowing down to roll through the streets that were deserted at a little after five-thirty in the morning. There were two gas stations, a general store, and a church spire showing above a cluster of houses.

In the other direction, the lake was still pewter-colored in the dawn. Before last night, Megan had been excited about coming here, had looked forward to it. Now she didn't know how she felt.

Behind her, Sandy stirred. "Where are we? Is there any place open to get something to eat?"

"We'll be at Grandpa's cottage in another twenty minutes," Mrs. Collier assured him. "He'll feed us. It's a pretty lake, isn't it? You'll have fun here."

Fun. The word was jarring, after what had happened last night. After they'd had to leave home without telling Annie they were leaving. Annie would be hurt, as hurt as Megan knew she would be if the situation were reversed. She didn't want to hurt Annie. Annie was the closest friend she'd ever had.

The air was cool and pine-scented as the road left the water and plunged into a forest of evergreens. Megan sat up straighter. In spite of her anxiety, she was hungry, too, and she looked forward to seeing Grandpa Davis and the lake up close.

"Watch for a red mailbox," her mother instructed, and then, "There it is! We turn here!"

Sandy glanced over his shoulder. "It's quite a ways from town, isn't it?"

"Six miles," his mother confirmed. "Too far to walk, but Grandpa goes in once a week for groceries and supplies."

There wasn't much of anything else to go to town for, Megan thought. She hadn't seen a movie theater or a bowling alley, or anything like that for entertainment. She wondered if there were any other kids living on the lake. A friend like Annie would be wonderful, but Annie probably would never forgive her. Not unless she could come up with a powerful excuse for having simply disappeared overnight.

The trees around them thinned, and they saw the lake again.

Now the sun was red in the eastern sky, and it tinted the surface of the water a shifting pink; on the far side, the forest remained black and seemingly impenetrable.

"The second driveway, Dad said. Ah, there it is." The car swung to the right, and they went a short distance before coming to a small clearing.

The cottage was nothing special, just a frame building with peeling white paint and dark red shutters. If there hadn't been an old car in the yard, Megan would have thought it was deserted. Beyond it, there was a narrow strip of pale, sandy beach with several outcroppings of dark rock, and beyond that, black on the pink-tinged water, an island.

Megan's heartbeat quickened. An island? It was only a little one, but it was so close to land that surely she could get out there. She wondered if Grandpa had a boat. There was something mysterious and special about an island.

Mrs. Collier let the car roll almost to the screened porch that ran the entire length of the cottage, then turned off the ignition. In the silence they heard a frog croaking, and far out on the lake, an outboard motor.

"Well, we're here. We might as well get out," Mrs. Collier said, and Megan wondered if she imagined the quaver in her mother's voice.

# *three*

MEGAN'S UNEASINESS deepened as they got out of the car. The early-morning air was chilly and out across the lake something gave a wild, sad cry. A loon? Hadn't one of Grandpa's letters said something about the loons?

Obviously Grandpa Davis wasn't expecting them. If he'd known they were coming, he'd have come out to meet them by this time, for he would surely have heard the car.

Mom was uneasy as well as exhausted, Megan thought. That's why she was acting so oddly—fumbling with her seat belt, groping for her purse, and then having difficulty in finding the key for the trunk so they could take out their luggage.

Sandy looked around with interest. "This is a neat place," he said. "Megan, did you see the islands?"

"Is there more than one?" She turned to stare out over the slate-colored water, which was already losing its pink tinge as the sun rose higher in the sky.

"Yeah. There's the one right off that way, and then there're a couple more farther on down the lake. One of them's so little maybe it's only a big rock. Gosh, I'm starved! Where's Grandpa?"

"Maybe you'd better carry one of these bags over to the porch, and knock on the door," Mrs. Collier suggested. Her voice didn't sound quite right, either.

Sandy had his fist raised toward the cottage door when it suddenly opened and Grandpa Davis stood there in a pair of old flannel pajamas, his graying hair standing in uncombed wisps. He blinked, and his jaw sagged momentarily. "Well, I'll be darned! I didn't expect you folks for another couple of weeks!"

Megan glanced at her mother. Though she was smiling, it wasn't her usual open smile.

"I hope it's all right, Dad. There wasn't any way to call you. I'll explain later. We're all starved. I hope you've got something to eat."

"Sure, sure. Come on in." Grandpa was a tall man with wide shoulders and hips narrow enough so his pajama pants sagged. He hitched them up with one hand. "Give me a chance to get dressed, and we'll mix up a batch of sourdough pancakes, how about that? Got some real maple syrup to go on 'em. Bet you kids never tasted any real maple syrup, just that cheap stuff they bottle these days. Sandy, I didn't exactly get things ready for you yet, but I figured you'd have the little bedroom in the back, there, and Megan and your mom could share the front bedroom. Take the bags through that door, boy, and give me a few minutes."

His right foot was in a cast, and it made a clumping sound on the wooden floor as he moved away.

Megan hauled the heavy suitcase through the doorway her grandfather had indicated. The cottage sure wasn't fancy, she thought. Probably they'd spend most of their time outside, on the beach or in the woods. Or maybe on those little islands.

The living room was small, with a stone fireplace and old, comfortable furniture. No rugs, just a bare wood floor, and not the polished kind, either; it was painted dark brown.

The bedroom was so tiny Megan couldn't see anywhere to put the suitcase except on the bed. There was a dresser and a chair, and that was all. Not even enough room on the floor for Annie's sleeping bag, unless they moved the chair out into the living room. If Sandy's room was smaller, he must have a single bed like the one she'd glimpsed through Grandpa's bedroom door.

Then her attention was caught by the view through the window facing the lake; she swung the suitcase onto the bed and gazed out over the water.

So quickly it changed as the sun rose! There were blue tints now in the gray of the placid surface. She could make out separate pine trees and a lone white-barked birch on the nearest island, and in spite of her uneasiness, she felt a tingle of eagerness. This was heightened by the sight of a rowboat drawn up in the shadow of the pines directly in front of the cottage. A way to get to the island!

"It's going to be fun, isn't it?" her mother asked from behind her.

"Not as much fun as if Annie had come with us, the way we planned," Megan said. "What's she going to think?"

For a moment her mother's throat worked, as if she

found speaking difficult. Then she swallowed. "I'm sorry, honey. It couldn't be helped."

"Why not? What's wrong? What happened? Why did we have to leave in the middle of the night, as if we'd done something wrong?"

Her mother had always talked openly to Megan; when there were questions, they had been answered. This time, however, it was as if a door had closed between them, shutting Megan out, though Mrs. Collier gave her a hug as she turned away from the window. "Later, honey. Come on, let's get some of those sourdough pancakes Grandpa makes."

Sandy was emerging from his room as they came out of theirs. "There's a boat, Megan, and a canoe! Did you see it? Wow, we can be Indians, or voyagers! We can explore the whole lake, and even the woods on the other side!"

"You don't want to wander too far and get lost," Mrs. Collier cautioned.

Grandpa appeared, still stuffing his shirttails into his trousers. "Now that's a fine way to talk, from someone who ran wild when she was a little girl. Brown as an Indian, she got, every year," he told the children. "And she picked berries and swam, and we hardly saw her from breakfast time until supper because she was out in the woods. Only reason she came home then, I guess, was because she ran out of food. Couldn't carry enough to keep her going past suppertime."

He chuckled and led the way into the kitchen, which was crowded with four of them in it. There was a tiny table covered with a plastic tablecloth, and four chairs, and cupboards made of knotty pine. Grandpa opened a door and took down a bowl.

"Megan and Sandy are city kids, Dad," Mrs. Collier said. "They don't know about the woods and the wilds."

"Well, this country's safer than the city these days," Grandpa said, and began mixing pancakes.

Megan waited tensely for her mother to explain their early arrival. She thought her grandfather was waiting, too; he was more relaxed about it, but he gave his daughter uneasy glances from time to time. He cooked pancakes until they'd all had their fill: light and fluffy and delicious with the real maple syrup and a chunk of butter atop each stack.

Sandy leaned back at last, patting his stomach with satisfaction. "Boy, I may get fat this summer."

"No, you'll run it off, same as your mother did," Grandpa predicted.

Sandy hesitated, then blurted out what Megan was thinking. "Mom, are you going to tell us now what this is all about? How come we're here early and everything?"

Grandpa seemed to nod very faintly. "You must have driven all night, Karo, to get here before I was even out of bed."

Megan held her breath. Now she'd know, she thought.

Only her mother didn't reply directly. She rose and began to clear the table. "It's a long story. And I did drive all night. I need to sleep a while before I'm up to it, I think. Why don't you kids go explore a little? This isn't where I grew up, but it's a lot like it. You'll have fun here, I know."

Fun? Megan wondered. All the happy anticipation she'd felt about coming here had disappeared during the night. Sandy gave her a look that suggested he was going to go along with the situation, at least for the moment.

"Yeah, let's go look around," he said. "Can we take the boat out, Grandpa? And the canoe?"

"The boat's safe enough, you couldn't turn it over if you tried. Just be sure the oars don't float away from you. You'd better practice with the canoe in shallow water at first; if you stand up in it, it'll dump you. You can both swim, though, can't you?"

"They've only done it in a pool," Mrs. Collier said.

"Water's water. Pool or a lake, swimming's the same. Actually, there are life jackets hanging on the tree there; be a good idea to wear them when you're on the water, just to be on the safe side. The paddles are under the canoe," Grandpa added, and Sandy was off at a trot, letting the screen door slam behind him.

Under other circumstances, Megan would have been right behind him. As it was, though, she was too worried to enjoy herself. It wasn't like her mother to act as if Megan and Sandy hadn't even asked her those important questions.

It was chilly, and she decided to get a sweater from the suitcase in the bedroom. She heard the murmur of voices from the kitchen as she searched for it, and then the words came more clearly as she returned to the living room.

"I didn't know what to do," Mrs. Collier said, "except run to you," and Megan came to a halt, heart thudding. Her mother sounded as if she were about to cry.

Clearly they thought both children had left the cottage. It was eavesdropping to stay there and listen, yet Megan couldn't help it. She felt as if she were rooted to the floor, her fingers numb on the sweater buttons.

Grandpa's voice, too, was serious. "What did you tell the kids?"

"I haven't told them anything yet. I didn't want to frighten them."

"You don't think you scared them by taking off in the middle of the night, before school was out for the summer? With no explanations?" Grandpa asked.

Megan felt the numbness spread through her body, accompanied by a chill that the sweater didn't help.

"You saw Sandy. He's tickled to be out early, and to be here."

"I saw Megan, too. I think you've scared her, Karo." It sounded strange; everyone except Grandpa called her mother Karen—he never did. When he wrote letters to her, he addressed them *Dear Daughter* or *Hi, Honey*. "Megan's a bright little thing. You're going to have to tell her something, or she'll be more worried than if she knows the truth."

"What? How can I explain, without *really* upsetting her? Maybe . . . it'll be all right, it will die down again and we can get on with our lives. . . ." There was a note of desperation Megan had never heard in her mother's voice.

"Die down again, the way it did eight years ago? Sooner or later, honey, the kids are going to have to know the truth."

Eight years ago? What had happened eight years ago? Megan wondered. There was no time to dwell on the question. She was holding her breath until her chest ached, waiting for the reply.

"Not yet," Mrs. Collier said, and it sounded as if she were pleading. "We were all right for eight years. . . ."

"Sure you were," Grandpa said, and though he didn't sound accusing—in fact was gentle, even tender—Megan thought he was trying very hard to convince her mother of something. "You moved how many times since then? Twelve? Fifteen? Every time you got spooked, you moved to a new town, a new job. The kids changed schools. Had to make new friends. That's hard on kids, Karo."

"Maybe not as hard as being as afraid as I am."

There, she'd put it into words, confirming Megan's suspicions. Why? Megan wondered, trembling. What could make a grown-up like her mother speak in this unsteady voice, make her admit to fear?

"Kids are tough, honey. If they know what the score is, they'll work with you, do what needs to be done. Tell 'em."

"But I lied to them, Daddy." There was something that made Megan's heart ache, in the way her mother was calling Grandpa *Daddy*. As if she were still a little girl instead of an adult, as if he could kiss her hurts and make them better. Until today, Megan had never heard her call him *Daddy*.

Yet it was her mother's words that really mattered. They were words that rocked Megan's whole world because they were so shocking.

"I've tried to teach them to be honest, not to tell lies. How can I admit to them now that *I've* been dishonest with *them?*"

"I expect the best thing," Grandpa said, and Megan heard the sounds of more coffee being poured into their mugs, and the scrape of the pot as it was being replaced on the stove, "is to explain why. They'll understand. They'll see why you had to do it."

"Maybe," her mother said, not sounding convinced. "But then they'll be afraid, too. They're so young. . . . Oh, Daddy, I'm tired. So tired. I've got to sleep for a few hours, anyway, and then I'll think about what to do. . . ."

A chair scraped on the kitchen floor, and Megan's paralysis was broken. She fled out the front door, closing the screen silently so as not to reveal that she'd been listening, her mother's words pounding in her ears.

*I lied to them, Daddy.*

About *what*, Megan wondered desperately. And *why?*

# *four*

SANDY HAD taken off his shoes and socks and rolled up his jeans, and was shoving on the bow of the rowboat, trying to get it into the water. He looked around at her, grinning. "Come on, help me! Let's row out to the island!"

Megan stared at her brother, swallowing painfully, wanting to believe she'd imagined the conversation she'd just overheard between her mother and her grandfather. Yet she knew she *hadn't* imagined it.

She wanted to strike out, to defend herself somehow, and Sandy was the only one she could attack. "Are you really that stupid, that all you want to do is go see an island?"

Astonished, Sandy stopped pushing on the boat and straightened up. "What's the matter with you?"

Tears stung Megan's eyes. "Don't you realize there's something horribly wrong?"

Sandy licked his lips uncertainly. "What?"

"Driving all night to get here, when Grandpa didn't even know we were coming, not telling Annie or anyone. . . . And Mom won't talk about it, won't tell us why. . . ."

"Well, yeah, but . . . Well, we're here, aren't we, and there's this neat island right out there, and . . . Megan? Do you know what's going on?"

She blinked, then wished she hadn't, because the tears spilled over and she had to wipe at them angrily with the back of one hand.

Sandy took a step toward her. "Hey, what is it? Are we in some kind of trouble or something?"

He looked so alarmed that she wished she hadn't said what she had. He was, after all, only ten. And whatever was happening, it wasn't his fault.

"I don't know. Mom was talking to Grandpa. I didn't hear all of it," she admitted shamelessly, "but she's scared of something. I think she told him what it is, or maybe he already knew. He told her to tell us, and she said she couldn't. She said . . ." Megan gulped, wondering belatedly if she should be dumping this on her younger brother, but he'd never let her stop now. "She said she'd taught us to be honest, so how could she tell us now that she's lied to us."

"Mom?" Sandy asked, incredulous. "Mom lied? About what?"

"I don't know about what! She said . . ." Megan struggled to remember the exact words. "She said, 'Maybe it would die down again'—she said *again*—'so we could get on with our lives,' and Grandpa said, 'You mean the way it did eight years ago?' and Mom said, 'We were all right for eight years.' And she said she was scared."

Sandy was looking scared now, too. "Eight years? What happened eight years ago?"

"I don't know. Nobody said. I can't remember that far back. I was only three years old."

"And I was only two." Sandy looked toward the cottage uncertainly. "You think Grandpa knows what it is? Maybe he'll explain."

"I don't think so. He acted like it was up to her. And it didn't sound to me as if she was going to tell us anything." Megan heard the quaver in her own voice and tried to steady it. "He said how many times we'd moved and had to change schools, and that it was hard on us. And that she'd probably scared us already, and she said we couldn't be as afraid as she is."

Sandy licked his lips again. "I didn't think mothers got scared of anything except . . . big, serious things."

"I didn't either. It scares me, too."

"What are we going to do, then?"

He meant, what was *Megan* going to do. She was the oldest, it was up to her to make the first move. Only she had no idea of what she could do. "Mom said she'd explain later. I'll ask her again, when we're alone. After she's had some sleep, maybe."

She didn't really believe that. Oh, she'd ask, but she didn't think her mother was going to tell her. And that was scarier than knowing the terrible secret, whatever it was.

Sandy dug his toes into the beach sand. "Well, if we can't do anything about it anyway, why let it wreck our whole vacation? Come on, let's go out to the island and see what it's like, OK?"

Megan supposed they might as well. Standing here in front of the cottage wasn't going to change anything. Exploring the island was spoiled now, because she couldn't stop thinking about her mother and why they were here. On the other hand, Sandy had a point. And what *could* they do about any of it?

"Grandpa said we're supposed to wear these," Sandy said, lifting down the bright orange life jackets from where they hung on nails in a tree. "I don't know why; we both know how to swim."

"It's farther across the lake than across the pool at home," Megan murmured, slipping her arms through the shoulder straps and fastening the ones across her chest. "We'd better do like he says."

She bent to take off her own shoes and socks, leaving them sitting on the edge of the beach in the scrubby grass. Then she joined her strength to Sandy's; they shoved the boat until it floated, and they hurriedly climbed in before it could get away. Sandy fitted the oars into the oarlocks and said, "I'll row."

"You'd better turn around, then," Megan told him. "You're supposed to sit facing the back of the boat."

"How'm I going to see where I'm going?" Sandy wanted to know.

"I don't know, but that's how they do it in the movies. You sit in the middle seat, with your back to the bow, and you go like this." She demonstrated with arm movements.

"OK, if you say so." Sandy tried it out, sending the little boat back to nose the shore. "This isn't going to work. How do I turn it around?"

"I think you row with one oar first, and that makes it turn."

It took a little maneuvering, but finally they were heading toward the island. Megan was glad Sandy was taking the first turn at rowing; after watching him struggle with it, she wouldn't feel quite such a klutz when she did it herself. Halfway across to the island, Sandy paused to rest. "It's harder work than it looks. You want to try it?"

"Sure," Megan said. They moved carefully to exchange places; the boat rocked, and then Megan gripped the oars and dipped them into the water and pulled.

"Maybe if you don't dip them quite so deep," her brother suggested, and she tried again, sort of skimming the surface, then experimenting until she began to get the hang of it.

Sandy was right; it *was* harder than it looked, and the island was farther away, too. Finally Sandy called out, "We're there!" and the last pull on the oars nosed them against, not sand, but rock.

"Wait," Sandy cried, "I'll get out with the rope and tie it to that little tree. There's no beach to pull it up on."

Since she had rowed the last part of the way, Megan hadn't seen the island up close until she clambered out after her brother. It was made of pinkish-gray rock formed in layers; some of them jutted out more than other layers, forming steps or shallow caves. There were scattered pines and a few birch trees that seemed to grow out of the rock itself, and walking was tricky because mostly the rock wasn't flat but rounded, occasionally dropping off sharply as much as five or six feet to the surrounding water.

Enough time had passed so that the sun was well up now. The lake was a brilliant blue, reflecting the sky overhead, and the water was so clear they could see well down into it; could see the pinkish rocks below the surface and tell where it was deep, and where it was shallow enough for wading.

"Hey, this is neat!" Sandy exclaimed, scrambling up one of the rocky "stairways" to a higher boulder. "See how little the cottage looks from here!"

Megan had been distracted enough so that for a few minutes she'd forgotten the cottage, and her mother, and the terrible secret, whatever it was.

"Come on," Sandy called, "let's see what the rest of it's like!"

He was off on all fours to the top of the slope, where he vanished down the other side with a whoop of delight.

Megan stared across the water. The cottage no longer looked shabby, because she couldn't see the peeling paint. Nothing moved over there. Her gaze swung down the lake, toward town. There were several more islands, smaller than this one, including one that was no more than a rock the size of their car with a single bush growing out of it. In the other direction, up the lake, a thin column of smoke rose from a log cabin barely visible through the pines. There *were* neighbors, then. She wondered if they had any kids, and then she thought about Annie, and once more tears made her eyes smart.

"Hey, Megan! Look what I've found!" Sandy shouted, and she turned to follow him up the sloping rock, which felt cool and rough beneath her hands and knees. Her brother had crossed to the far side of the island—a distance no greater than moving across an ordinary street at home. He was standing below her in a tiny cove, lined with a narrow strip of sandy beach just wide enough to walk on.

"It'll be a great place to swim!" he called up to her. "The rock goes out so the water's not very deep here; we can bring the boat over on this side to unload supplies!"

"Supplies?" Megan echoed, starting down toward him, carefully so as not to slip and slide all the way into the water before she could stop.

"Sure! We'll bring picnic stuff, and maybe books to read—there's almost a cave, too!"

Megan slid the last few yards on her bottom; the sand was pleasantly warm beneath her bare feet, and very soft and clean. "How can there be *almost* a cave?" she demanded.

"Well, it hasn't got any sides, but see how the rock sticks out enough so we could sit under there if it rained, and not get wet? We could even sleep under there, if we brought sleeping bags."

"Mom'd never let us," Megan said automatically, but she, too, felt the magic of the place. If only there weren't some awful thing hanging over their family, she could fall in love with this spot.

"I'll bet Grandpa would think it was OK. He said it was safer up here in the woods than in town, didn't he? We'll ask him first, and he can work on Mom. Let's go see what else there is here. The island isn't very wide, but it's about four times as long. Maybe there's another beach."

There wasn't, but the island was enchanting. So private, Megan thought, a place to come and dream or think or cry, if she felt like crying.

She would never have had that final thought before last night. Before her good, safe life was disrupted, before her mother had become so frightened of something that she'd run away from it. Before Megan knew that her mother had lied to her about whatever it was. Her mother, who never lied about anything, not even her age, the way some mothers did.

They were halfway back to the mainland when the idea suddenly came to her.

"I know one thing that happened eight years ago, when I was three and you were two," Megan said slowly, her heart rate accelerating.

"What?" Sandy demanded.

"Eight years ago was when Daddy died."

Sandy's face was blank. "What could that have to do with anything that's happening now?"

"I don't know," Megan admitted. Yet she was remembering how her mother always acted, reluctant to talk about their father, as if it still hurt to do so. Could there be a connection between Daddy's death and Mom's fear now?

She fell silent, and pulled awkwardly on the oars, taking them back to Grandpa's cottage.

## *five*

THEY MUST have been gone longer than it had seemed, for when they entered the cottage they could smell something good—lunch was cooking.

Sandy bounded into the kitchen and looked hopefully at the kettle on the stove. "What is it?"

"Homemade vegetable soup," Grandpa said. "I thought you'd be turning up soon. Wash up, and sit down."

Megan stood in the doorway, staring at the table, which was set with three bowls and three glasses. "Who isn't eating?" she said, and in her own ears her voice sounded strange, almost frightened, though she wasn't sure why.

"I'm not. I have to go," Mrs. Collier said.

Megan turned and saw her mother coming out of the little bedroom they were to have shared, pulling on her sweater. She certainly didn't look rested; her eyes were puffy and smiling was an effort, though she hugged Megan and tried to seem normal.

"I have to be gone for a few days. You'll have a good time here. Don't worry about me."

The fear inside of Megan deepened, grew stronger. "Where are you going?" There was a tremor in her legs, and her mouth was so dry it was an effort to speak.

"I'll tell you about it when I get back, all right? No, honest, Dad, I'm not hungry. I don't want anything to eat."

Grandpa had ladled out a bowl of soup for Sandy. Now he picked up a plastic bag from the counter. "I made you a sandwich to take with you, anyway. You'll get hungry sooner or later."

"Oh. Well, OK. Thank you," Mrs. Collier said, accepting the bag and taking her arm away from Megan. "Give me a kiss, Sandy, and remember, Grandpa's the boss."

Sandy's freckled face showed concern. "Where are you going, Mom?"

"I'm not sure yet. I'll let you know." She bent to rest a hand on his shoulder and kiss him on the forehead, then kissed Megan as well. "I'll be in touch."

"But Mom . . ." Megan's protest sounded squeaky.

"You'll be perfectly safe here with Grandpa. Have fun," she said, and then kissed her father, too, and was gone.

Megan watched woodenly through the kitchen window as the car backed and turned in the side yard, then vanished through the trees. Safe? Wasn't that a peculiar thing for her mother to say, unless for some reason they were in danger?

"Eat up," Grandpa said, trying to sound cheerful and not quite making it. "Vegetable soup. Got everything in it but the kitchen sink. Keep you going until suppertime.

Of course, if you get too bad off in the meantime, there are some oranges and bananas to stave off starvation."

Megan wanted desperately to ask him to explain what was going on. He certainly knew more than she did. She felt abandoned; it wasn't fair for her mother to go away with no warning, without explaining, without giving Megan a chance to ask questions. Though resentment churned inside her, she couldn't quite put her feelings into words.

Besides, Grandpa probably wouldn't tell her anything anyway, not unless her mother had told him he could.

She took the chair beside Sandy, who was eagerly spooning up chunks of beef and carrots and potatoes and peas. He paused long enough to crumble crackers into the bowl, and then, after he'd eaten everything in front of him, handed up his dish for a refill. "Are there any kids to play with here, Grandpa?" he asked as he accepted seconds.

"Not that I know of. May be some in another couple of weeks, when the tourists start coming up from Minneapolis and Chicago for the summer. There's a string of cabins at the far end of the lake." Grandpa helped himself to crackers.

"Are we still going to be here a couple of weeks from now?" Sandy asked. His blue eyes were watchful, wary, and Megan went stiff, waiting for the answer.

"Well, your mom didn't say for sure, but I'd guess so. Maybe for the whole summer," Grandpa said quietly.

"The whole summer?" Sandy considered this, then grinned uncertainly. "I was going to be on a softball team at home. But I guess swimming's OK, too. The water's kind of cold, though. I waded in it."

"It'll warm up pretty good by July, they tell me. Not too warm, I hope. Bad for the fishing when it's too warm. Want to come along this afternoon, see if we can land ourselves enough bass for supper?"

"Sure," Sandy agreed with enthusiasm, then glanced at Megan. "You want to come, Megan?"

She shook her head. "No, thanks." How could he think about just having fun, when something was so obviously and horribly wrong? She realized Grandpa was watching her and added, "I'll find something to do. Read, maybe. I saw some books in the other room."

"Old, but some good ones. Left by a couple of generations of vacationers, I guess," Grandpa said. He sounded relieved that she wasn't making a fuss about her mother leaving so unexpectedly, and a part of her resented that, too, though she knew it wasn't his fault. He'd tried to talk his daughter into being honest with them.

It was strange to think of her mother as being *dis*honest. As if she'd suddenly become another person, not the mother Megan had known all her life.

It didn't seem to be bothering Sandy all that much. He finished his soup and crackers, drained his glass, and selected a banana for dessert. "We saw smoke from a log cabin up the lake. Who lives there?" he asked.

"Oh, that's our only neighbor at the moment. Haven't met him but once, when he was walking on the beach at sunset. Not a fisherman, I guess; I've never seen him out on the lake. Name's Nathan Jamison. Seems like a nice fella; writes books, I understand. Came here for the peace and quiet."

There was only one thing wrong with peace and quiet, Megan reflected after Sandy and Grandpa had departed with their fishing tackle in the rowboat. It gave you too much time to think.

Ordinarily she wouldn't have minded. She enjoyed daydreaming. She could imagine all kinds of exciting adventures with the horse she would have—a palomino, with a flowing blond mane and tail, that could run like the wind. Sometimes she imagined meeting a faceless boy who would have a horse of his own—a black stallion—who would race with her on a broad, sandy beach, a boy who would think she was pretty. It was silly, but it was kind of fun, too.

Only now she felt neither silly nor like having fun. She felt, in fact, like crying. She and her mother had always been so close. Why had Mom shut her out?

Megan looked through the books on the brown painted shelves in one corner of the living room. Grandpa was right; they were sure old. Zane Grey westerns, and a whole shelf by someone named Grace Livingston Hill, which appeared upon investigation to be old-fashioned romances, and some *National Geographics* with pictures of naked natives in Africa. The magazines were so old that she didn't recognize the name of the country where they lived; no doubt the name had been changed years ago.

She didn't really want to read. She walked onto the porch and stared out over the lake. Grandpa and Sandy were tiny figures in the boat on the water. She felt a moment of envy that they could put aside worry and just enjoy themselves. Why wasn't she like that?

She went slowly down the steps and onto the beach. If they hadn't taken the boat, she'd row back out to the island; it seemed a place of refuge, a place where trouble might not be able to follow her.

What about the canoe?

Megan walked over to it and ran a hand along its bright red surface. Though she'd never paddled a canoe, she'd seen it done in the movies often enough. Maybe if her father had lived, he'd have taught her how . . .

No. She remembered now, Mom had said he wasn't an outdoorsman, so he probably hadn't gone canoeing.

Well, it hadn't looked hard. Grandpa had said to be careful, because it tipped over easily, but even if it did, she could swim, couldn't she?

Out on the lake, she could see the spot of bright orange that was Sandy's life jacket. She supposed she'd better wear one, too, just in case.

Tentatively, Megan lifted the edge of the canoe. It wasn't all that heavy; it rolled over, right-side-up, revealing the paddles that had been hidden beneath it. It was certainly easier to move into the water than the rowboat had been; easy enough so that it almost got away from her, and she took a couple of quick steps—wetting the bottoms of her pants legs—to catch it. Put the paddles in first, then shove off into the very shallow water, and get in—carefully, carefully!

Did she need both paddles? Unless there were two people in the canoe, she'd only need one, but she recalled what Grandpa had said about losing one. Maybe it wouldn't hurt to have them both, just in case.

The canoe seemed fragile and unstable, compared to the rowboat. However, even though she felt awkward and insecure, she liked the way the slender vessel glided over the surface of the lake, as light as one of the little white butterflies that fluttered along the shore.

If she just remembered not to move suddenly, she didn't think she'd overturn the canoe. At first she moved parallel to the shore, in water where she could see the bottom only a few feet below her, and then she grew braver and turned the bow out toward the island.

Paddling the canoe wasn't quite as simple as she'd supposed. She wasn't sure how those people in the movies dipped into the water on only one side and managed to go straight ahead; when she tried it, she went in circles.

And it was hard to lift the paddle out of the water, moving it from side to side, in order to go straighter. There must be some trick to this, she decided.

Nevertheless, she was heading toward the island, which was where she wanted to go. And in one way it was easier in the canoe than in the boat; you sat facing in the direction you were traveling.

She had to learn some new maneuvers to work her way around to the far side of the island, to the little cove with the sandy beach. There, it was easy to grasp the prow and haul the canoe up onto the sand, where it would stay until she was ready to leave.

She explored the entire island again, which didn't take very long because it wasn't very big, and gradually felt a sense of peace overtake her. It was so quiet. The sun was warm on her bare arms and face, and the slight breeze was cool.

It was only when she stood at the highest point on the pinkish-gray rocks and looked toward the cottage on the mainland that she came back to reality.

The cottage sat looking deserted in the afternoon sunshine. There was nothing moving.

Safe, her mother had said. They would be safe here with Grandpa.

It would never have occurred to Megan that they were *not* safe if her mother hadn't said that.

Was that why they'd run away from home late at night and come here? Because they were *not safe at home?*

But what was the danger?

Far up the beach, two tiny figures stirred. A man— their neighbor in the log cabin—was walking on the beach with a dog. The man threw a stick into the water, and the dog swam out to retrieve it.

She wished she had a dog. Watching the pair, the man throwing the stick, the dog plunging into the lake after it, made her feel lonely. She wished Annie were here. Annie would help her figure out what was going on. Annie would make her laugh.

She didn't want to watch the man and his dog. Seeing them only made her feel more lonely. Usually she and her brother agreed on things, but Sandy didn't seem to be taking this matter seriously. Not as seriously as *she* did. Look at the way he'd gone off fishing with Grandpa.

An inner sense of fairness murmured that since there was nothing Sandy could do about their situation, there was no reason for him not to go fishing. Megan pushed it away. She didn't want to forgive him for deserting her to worry by herself.

Megan turned, and slipped and slid her way back down to the little cove. There, with the sun gently warming her face, she sat on the soft sand and cried a little.

Wishing Sandy had not gone fishing. Wishing her father had not died so there would be someone else to turn to. Wishing her mother had not gone away and left them here. Wishing that, at the very least, someone would tell her what was wrong.

Why were they safe here, when apparently they had not been at home?

What if her mother were wrong? What if they were not safe at all, from whatever it was that threatened them?

## six

AS GRANDPA cooked supper—fish, fried potatoes and salad—Megan set the table. Tentatively, she tried to sound him out on their situation.

"Do you know where Mom went?" she asked, so nervous that she didn't dare look directly at him.

The fish sizzled in the pan, and he adjusted the heat under it. "She didn't tell me," he replied. "Shall we open a can of peaches for dessert? No fresh ones available yet."

"Sure," Megan agreed. "Did she tell you how long she'd be gone?"

"She didn't tell me much of anything, honey. Only that she wanted me to keep you kids here for a while. You like it here, don't you?"

The cast on his foot made a clumping sound as he moved

to the sink, and Megan suppressed a spurt of guilt, wondering if his injured foot still hurt. Cooking for three made him stand up longer than cooking for one, but she didn't know how to do much so she could help him.

"I . . . guess so. Except for not having any other kids around. My friend Annie was going to come. . . ." She couldn't help the prickle of tears behind her eyelids.

She swallowed. "Does it hurt to walk?"

"What? Oh, my foot? No, not any more. Hurt like sixty at first. It's just awkward." He raised his voice so it would carry to the back porch. "Sandy, you got the rest of those bass cleaned yet?"

Sandy came through the door carrying a pan with more fish. "We can't eat all of this tonight, can we? Even if we *are* starved?"

"No. Put what you have in those shallow pans and cover them with water, then stick them in the freezer inside the plastic bags I put out. That way, they'll taste like we just caught them when we get around to eating them."

Sandy clearly was pleased with himself. Grandpa had caught *more* bass, but Sandy had caught the biggest one. He was grinning until he saw his sister's face and remembered.

She felt another twinge of guilt at the way his pleasure evaporated when he saw her own expression. Yet why should she feel guilty? It wasn't her fault their mother had behaved so strangely, and she couldn't help being afraid.

She was as hungry as the other two, and ate her share of the fish and everything else. Yet she couldn't get her mind off their predicament.

There was no TV. Grandpa said there were too many

of those solid granite rocks and hills between them and the TV towers for the waves to get through. So they had to think of something else to do during the evenings.

"There are some old games on the shelf below the books," Grandpa said. "Checkers and Monopoly. I always listen to the news after supper on the radio. We have a local station, so that comes through all right."

"I think I'll take a walk before it gets dark," Megan said. She gave Sandy a look, and he followed her out onto the porch.

"We need to talk," she told him. "Grandpa's not going to give anything away. I asked him, and he doesn't know where Mom went or when she'll be back, he said."

"I know it," Sandy agreed, surprising her. "I tried to pump him, too, while we were fishing. He said it was up to Mom to tell us what she wants us to know. I thought that was lousy. It's not like we were little kids, or irresponsible or anything. But he said she's our mother, and it's her decision."

So Sandy was more seriously concerned than she'd thought. That ought to have made her feel better; but instead, Megan found it only made her own anxiety worse.

"We've got to figure it out for ourselves, then," she decided aloud.

"How? What can we do?"

"I don't know yet, but we'll have to try, anyway. What kind of thing would Mom be afraid of? What—or who— would she run away from and hide?"

Sandy's face was sober. "People usually do that when they've done something illegal, like stealing. Mom wouldn't ever steal! Would she?"

"No. If she'd stolen anything—from the office or someplace like that—we'd have something to show for it, wouldn't we? She'd have bought a new car, or new clothes, or even more groceries. Besides, I'll never believe she'd take anything she had no right to. Not after the way she's lectured us all our lives about being honest. There has to be something else."

What it could be, however, neither of them could figure out. If it wasn't illegal—like stealing—what did that leave?

"She's afraid. She said so," Megan mused, looking out over the lake, where the water was now smooth as glass, mirroring the dark trees on the far shore, and the pink tint of the sun on the clouds. "That means she's afraid of something, or someone. Who?"

"Not the police," Sandy said. "At least I don't think the police. Gosh, Megan, do you think she's been running away and hiding from someone for eight years?"

Megan didn't have to consider her answer; she'd already been thinking about it. "Maybe. Remember how many times we've moved? How many times Mom's told us it was because of her job? She never got a new job in the same town. We always went miles away, so we could never see any of our friends again."

"And she didn't even want us to write to any of them," Sandy added.

Megan glanced at him sharply. "You're right. She didn't, did she? When I was going to write to Joanie Miller, after we moved the last time, she said maybe it would be better if we just made new friends where we were, instead of staying hung up on the past." A lump formed in her throat. "I suppose that means I'll never be able to explain to Annie, even if I knew how."

"Mom's not here now. She wouldn't know if you wrote to Annie."

Megan's heart began to race. "I owe Annie a letter, at least. Don't I?"

"If my best friend moved away, I'd expect him to say good-bye, anyway," Sandy agreed.

It didn't solve the problem, of course. They were no nearer to solving the riddle than they'd been in the beginning, but it made Megan feel better to decide that she should write to Annie.

"I'll do it tonight," she said. "And we'll walk out to the mailbox on the road to mail it, first thing in the morning."

"Maybe there'll be something for us, from Mom," Sandy said hopefully.

"Not tomorrow, she only left today. Tomorrow will be too soon. I hope she isn't gone long."

"Hey! The news is over. You kids want to play Monopoly?" Grandpa called through the screen door.

"Sure, why not?" Sandy was already moving in that direction, and Megan followed. She'd write the letter after the game. She couldn't tell Annie *why* they had moved, but she could explain that she hadn't wanted it to happen that way, and that she was sorry Annie hadn't been able to share their vacation as they'd planned.

Some vacation, she reflected as Sandy set up the board and began to sort out the game pieces on the kitchen table. Somehow, she had to find out the truth of what was behind this hasty trip to the lake, behind the secrecy. She was eleven, not a baby, and she had a right to know, whatever it was.

THE BRIGHT morning sun glittered on the lake beyond her window the next morning as Megan licked the flap on the envelope and sealed it. Her letter was brief, no more than enough to assure Annie that she was sorry they'd left in the night and she hoped they'd see one another again some day. She hadn't really explained the matter, because after several tries she could see that it sounded worse, not knowing, than simply letting it slide by as a peculiarity on the part of her mother.

She had found stationery and a pen in the folder her mother had left behind, containing everything that hadn't fit into one suitcase. Now Megan looked through it hoping there would be stamps, too. Probably Grandpa had stamps, but somehow Megan didn't want to ask him. She wondered uneasily if he, too, would advise against writing to Annie, maybe even forbid her to do it.

Ah, there were the stamps, mixed in with stuff like Megan's and Sandy's vaccination records and the car insurance papers. It looked as if Mom had grabbed everything out of her desk and crammed it into the folder without sorting it. That in itself showed how urgent the need had been to leave quickly, because ordinarily Mrs. Collier was neat and well organized.

Megan stuck on the stamp, then put the letter in the pocket of her sweatshirt, hoping Grandpa wouldn't ask where she was going.

Grandpa, however, wasn't in the living room when she left her tiny bedroom.

"He's going fishing again," Sandy announced. "I told him I didn't want to go today; I figured we'd go back out to the island and see what it would take to build us a clubhouse or something. We'll have to take the canoe; he's got the rowboat."

"OK. After we mail the letter to Annie," Megan said, relieved.

It took about ten minutes to reach the mailbox. They put the letter in and put up the flag so the rural carrier would pick it up. By the time they got back to the cottage, it was warm enough for them to get rid of their sweatshirts before they put on their life jackets.

"This is trickier than the boat," Megan warned. "You get in and sit down with one paddle, and I'll shove us off. You paddle on the left, and I'll paddle on the right, and we should go straight."

It wasn't quite that easy, because Sandy dipped his paddle more deeply and firmly than she did hers, so they tended to swing to the left, but they decided it was simply a matter of practice.

Sandy stood up as they nosed into the tiny cove on the far side of the island, and the next thing they knew, they were spluttering and coming up for air, their hair plastered to their heads, soaking wet.

"I guess that isn't the way you're supposed to do it," Sandy gasped. "Wow, the water's cold! I thought these life jackets were supposed to keep you from going under!"

Megan grabbed the canoe, which was easing away from shore, and began to push it out onto the sand. She, too, was gasping from the shock of the icy water. "I don't think that applies when you go in head first. You came back up, didn't you? Come on, give me a hand getting the canoe up on the beach."

Sandy came over to help, still shivering in spite of the warm sun. "I told you, Megan. We should build a shelter and keep supplies over here for emergencies like this."

"A change of clothes?" she asked, satisfied that the canoe was safe, and wringing water out of her long hair.

"Why not? And food. So we wouldn't have to go home just because we get hungry." Sandy peeled off the life jacket, then turned and scrambled up the rock, leaving a wet trail on its pinkish-gray surface.

Home, Megan thought. The cottage wasn't home. Even Grandpa would only be there until his foot healed so he could go back to work. There wasn't any home now, anywhere.

Was that what Mom was doing, finding a new job and a new place to live in another strange town? For a moment anger replaced the fear she had been living with for the past couple of days. Anger toward her mother, who had somehow put them in this bleak position—again. Megan was sure that it was *again*, that this was part of a pattern she and Sandy simply hadn't been aware of before. Running and hiding; when was it going to end?

She thought of the letter to Annie, and the anger subsided into sadness, and a little shame, too. Whatever it was, her mother didn't want it any more than Megan did. Her fingers numb, she unfastened the life jacket and left it beside Sandy's, well above the water line.

"How about over there?" Sandy was asking as she reached the top of the rocky slope. Her hands no longer left wet marks on the stone, though her clothes continued to drip. "We could put some branches over the front of that cave to hide our stuff, and maybe we could even build a fire on the ledge in front of it and cook hot dogs or something like that."

To begin with, Megan moved sluggishly, her mind on their problems. But gradually she threw more energy into helping Sandy drag pine boughs from the surrounding trees—small ones, because they hadn't brought a knife to cut off the larger ones—until finally all she thought about was the shelter they were building.

It wasn't actually a cave, she supposed, because the sides were open, but the jutting, layered rock provided a roof overhead, and the pine boughs shielded them from the view of any passing fishermen on the water. Not that there were any, except Grandpa, and he was half a mile up the lake.

Their clothes and hair were completely dried by the time they shoved off in the canoe to return to shore. Grandpa was still fishing; he gave them a wave, and they waved back, until Megan said sharply, "Be careful, Sandy, you'll dump us again, and we don't know how to get back in this thing out here in deep water!"

"Oh, yeah, I forgot," Sandy said sheepishly. He took up his paddle again. "I'm glad Grandpa isn't nervous, like Mom. So he'll let us run around out here, and not keep fussing if he can't see us every minute."

Megan nodded as the canoe nosed toward the beach in front of the cottage. "Let's get something to eat, and then go and see if there's any mail. There *might* be something from Mom."

There wasn't, however. There was no mail at all, but the letter to Annie was gone. Megan wondered if she'd get the letter if Annie wrote back to her. She hadn't known what return address to put, and she hadn't wanted to ask Grandpa for fear he'd tell her not to mail her letter. All she had was the name of the town, Lakewood. The first time they went into the village, she'd try to find the post office and ask if they had anything for her.

The rowboat was back at the mainland. Grandpa greeted them with a grin as they entered the kitchen. "Bet you're starving, eh? I'm fixing up a stack of sandwiches, be ready in a minute. You should have come with me, Sandy, the fish were biting pretty good. I got two, and one of them was almost as big as the one you caught yesterday."

They joined him in buttering the bread, and didn't mention the snack they'd had before going to the mailbox.

Being out on the water increased their appetites, Megan decided; Sandy was right about keeping supplies out at their cave.

"You going fishing again this afternoon, Grandpa?" Sandy asked with his mouth full and a milky mustache that Mom would have objected to.

"Nope, thought I'd gather a little firewood. Evenings are still chilly enough so the fireplace is welcome. You kids want to help me, or have you got something else planned?"

"Well, if you aren't using the boat, I thought maybe we'd go back to the island. We're fixing up a cave. Would it be OK if we took some stuff to eat, and maybe a couple of blankets?"

Laugh wrinkles formed around Grandpa's eyes. "A cave, eh? I'd have liked to do that myself when I was your age. Sure, take some fruit, and there's some crackers and peanut butter if you want 'em. I don't know about blankets—I'm not sure we've got any spares—but there's a couple of old sleeping bags in that back closet. Help yourselves."

The rowboat had more room to carry things, even a lantern Grandpa said they wouldn't need at the house unless the electricity went off, which it never had done since he'd been here. He showed them how to use it safely, and even gave them a little box of waterproof matches.

The boat didn't glide over the water as easily as the canoe, but it was less likely to dump them into the lake. Rowing continued to be awkward. They thought they were getting a little better at it, though their arms and shoulders still ached by the time they'd crossed to the island.

They forgot that as soon as they arrived. It was fun, arranging their furnishings in the cave. They left the sleeping bags rolled up to lean against, and arranged the other supplies on an inner ledge that might have been made for the purpose.

It was so nice when they were finished that they hated to go home to the cottage for supper.

Grandpa had not only put in a supply of firewood, he'd made spaghetti. Tonight Sandy set the table while Megan sliced vegetables for a salad. Even that was a reminder that made her uneasy once more. It had all begun—at least as far as Megan was concerned—when Mom dropped the salad bowl and broke it. That bowl had been a treasured possession, yet Mom had scarcely noticed what she'd done.

She'd been upset, but not about breaking the bowl. And not about cutting her feet a little bit, either, Megan thought. Sandy said she'd been watching TV—the news, maybe— and she'd been startled and dropped the bowl. Only why? What could have been on the news that had anything to do with *them?*

Was she crazy, to think that was what had happened? Megan resolved to stay inside tonight and listen to the news with Grandpa.

Only there was nothing on the radio except things that were happening in distant places, to people she'd never heard of. She joined Sandy and Grandpa in a game of Monopoly they didn't have time to finish before they had to go to bed, but her mind kept wrestling with the riddle. What could Mom have heard on the TV news that would have frightened her so badly, when it apparently hadn't frightened anyone else?

The following morning, when Grandpa announced that he needed a few things from town, he took it for granted that they wanted to stay behind and ferry more supplies to the island. He'd come up with an old ice chest—though he said if they took cans of pop they could set them in the water and refrigerate them without needing any ice—and a little grate they could put across a couple of rocks to form a cooking surface. Sandy was full of plans for a weenie roast, and Grandpa said he'd bring back marshmallows, too.

It was too early to expect a reply from Annie, so Megan didn't ask if they could go with Grandpa into Lakewood. The island had worked a spell on her yesterday. She'd managed to forget how frightened she was, at least most of the time. So she couldn't wait to get back to it.

Her anticipation and pleasure were shattered, however, within moments of setting foot on the small beach. In fact, she was still hauling the boat ashore when Sandy's stunned voice brought her sharply around.

"Megan, look! Somebody's been here!"

And there was the evidence, plain to see: a bare footprint in the sand, bigger than either of their own.

## seven

MEGAN'S INITIAL REACTION was disappointment. Someone had invaded her own private territory!

"It's bigger than mine, but not adult-size," Sandy said, placing his own foot next to the footprint in the sand. "I thought these islands didn't belong to anybody. I mean, Grandpa didn't say we'd be trespassing if we built a club-house here."

Megan looked around. While it was true they didn't *own* the island, there had been no sign that anyone else ever visited it. Except for the man who was writing a book—the man who threw sticks for his dog—there weren't even supposed to be any other people living on the lake right now.

"Here's another one," Sandy announced, following the trail across the sand. The footprints vanished when he came to the rock. "I hope he didn't find our hideout! I hope he didn't mess up our stuff!"

He was off, first scrambling up the rock, then running toward their cave. Megan hurried after him. It wasn't fair that someone else should be here, in a place that *felt* like their own, not after they'd worked so hard to fix it up into a refuge, a place where they could almost forget what was happening in their lives on the mainland.

Every time Sandy came to a spot where sand lay over the rock, he paused to look for more footprints. Before they ever reached the cave, Megan knew they were going to find that it, too, had been discovered. Both of the prints her brother had found since they'd left the beach were headed in that direction.

Had someone watched them fixing it up, from the far shore where she could see only dark evergreens and a few contrasting birch trees? She stood for a moment, shading her eyes, but nothing moved on the opposite side of the lake.

"He's been here!" Sandy shouted, reaching the cave ahead of her. "He even came inside!"

Megan ducked her head to keep from bashing it on the rocky overhang. "He must have known it was a private place," she said bitterly. "He could see we have our stuff here."

"It doesn't look as if he took anything, though," Sandy said after a moment. "The food's all here, and the lantern and the sleeping bags."

"How did he get here?" Megan wondered aloud. "There was no boat. Our own little beach is the only place you can land with a boat unless you want to climb straight up the way we did the first time."

They didn't learn the answer to that until they returned

to their own boat. Sandy poked around and discovered that in the sand at the very end of the strip of beach, there was an indentation such as would be made by the bow of a canoe, and part of one footprint that hadn't been washed away by the waves.

"It's all spoiled now," Megan said, staring at the marks. "It was a special place, just for us, and he's spoiled it." She *needed* the island, needed a place of her own.

"He didn't actually hurt anything," Sandy pointed out. "Maybe it's another kid. Maybe it's someone to do things with."

"He went into our cave. He snooped," Megan said. "He could see it belonged to someone else." It was the only place that did belong to them, she thought. They had no home, they had been taken away from their friends, and even the cottage was a temporary place, one Grandpa had only rented until his foot healed.

"There are other islands," Sandy said after a moment of silence. "Why don't we go explore some of the other ones?"

This was the best one, Megan thought. You could tell that without ever stepping onto the others. But at least for now she didn't want to stay here. "OK. Let's go look," she agreed without enthusiasm. They had to do *something* to pass the time until their mother came back for them.

After they unloaded the supplies they'd brought, they visited four other islands. By the end of the day, they both had aching muscles and sore hands from using the oars. Though Megan was right about *their* island being the best, the others were interesting, too. They were all small; one was so tiny that it was all they could do to both fit on it at the same time. It had one scraggly juniper bush growing out of the single rock that formed it, and

Sandy laughingly announced that he was going to tie something to the top of the bush, claiming it for himself.

When they finally dragged home for supper, Megan picking a sliver out of her palm from her last stint with the oars, Sandy asked Grandpa about the islands.

"Well, I suppose they belong to somebody," he conceded, raising his voice to be heard over the sizzle of frying meat. "You kids ever have fresh side pork? Hardly ever see it anymore; they usually make bacon out of that cut these days. It was always one of my favorite meals, with boiled potatoes and cream gravy. And peas. I got some fresh peas to go with it."

"Somebody was on our island," Sandy said. "We found his footprints."

"That so? Wouldn't have thought Mr. Jamison would go out there; I've never even seen him in a boat, though there's a canoe goes with the cabin he rented. Fellow comes up weekends sometimes has an outboard, but he's older than I am, and all he ever does is fish. Get me some paper towels to drain this on, will you, Megan?"

She handed him the roll of towels. "Maybe we have another new neighbor."

"Could be. They'll start coming in droves, they tell me in town, soon as school is out. All the lakes around here, hundreds of people come up from the cities to vacation. Well, this person didn't steal your stuff, did he?"

"No. He went into our cave, though, and looked at it. We just wondered if the islands belonged to anybody."

"My guess is they probably belong to the state. They aren't big enough to build anything on, so most individuals wouldn't want them," Grandpa said.

"We went on one," Sandy told him, getting the milk out of the refrigerator, "that's barely big enough for both of us to stand on. You couldn't put anything bigger than a dollhouse on that."

Grandpa stirred the peas, chuckling as he began to dish them up. "Funny thing about islands, they fascinate most people. I knew you kids would enjoy these."

"I'm going to try to find something to make a flag to fly on the smallest one," Sandy said, "and maybe we'll have a ceremony and name it. Megan can share the big one with Bigfoot, or whoever left his prints there."

"There's a miniature American flag in the closet where you got the sleeping bags. Don't see any reason why you can't use that if you want it," Grandpa said. "I like to see a flag flying. Come on, let's eat."

They had the ceremony the following day. The flag was a bright spot of color fluttering in the breeze as they rowed away from it. Although Megan had told him that it was only ships that were christened with champagne, Sandy had insisted on popping open a can of 7-Up and pouring it over the juniper bush as he pronounced, "I now name you Sandy's Island," in formal tones. He wore a broad grin, and Megan wished that she felt as upbeat as he did.

His joy faded into alarm as soon as they rounded the end of the big island. "Megan! He's here again! He's *still here!*"

There was a yellow canoe leaning on its side on their small beach, as if it belonged there.

"We don't own the island, and maybe he's got as much right to come here as we have," Megan muttered, "but he's got no right to touch our stuff!"

"Who wants to touch your old stuff? It's just junk," the voice said loudly, over their heads.

Megan stopped in the act of drawing their rowboat up beside the yellow canoe.

The intruder stood on the top of the rocky ridge, a tall, skinny boy of perhaps twelve, with faded jeans that needed mending, and a shock of dark brown hair that fell over his forehead. He had eyes so dark they were nearly black, and a scowl twisted his rather attractive face.

"What're you doing on our island?" Sandy demanded, though he didn't sound as hostile as the stranger had.

"It's not your island," the boy countered. "My dad says these islands don't belong to anybody, so I've got as much right to be here as you do."

"But not to bother our stuff."

"I didn't take any of it." The boy swiped the hair back from his face. "None of it's worth taking, actually."

Megan tried to keep her voice carefully neutral. "Good. Then you won't get in our way." She started up the slope, right toward him. Because of the incline, she had to crawl, and she didn't know until she reached the top that he hadn't moved; he stood blocking her way, making her swerve aside.

Sandy, right behind her, stood up and faced the boy. "Stay out of our cave, then."

The boy was even taller than Megan had thought, a full head taller than she was. He made a snorting sound. "It's a baby's place. Little kid stuff. Why don't you build a real house?"

"Because we haven't got anything to build with," Sandy said. "It takes lumber and nails and hammers, and we don't have any."

The boy considered that. Some of the hostility went out of his thin face. "There's stuff at my dad's cabin," he said surprisingly. "The landlord tore down an old house and brought a load of lumber for firewood. Some of it's good enough to build out of, and nobody will care. It's just for the tenants to put in the fireplace. And Dad has saws and hammers, stuff like that. He's going to rebuild the porch steps, for part of the rent."

"I suppose you're an expert on building," Megan heard herself saying, and then wondered why she bothered with this boy she was obviously going to dislike.

"I know more than just cutting a few spruce branches and propping them over the opening to a cave. My dad used to have me help him build lots of things, before he moved out." The boy hesitated, then turned to gesture over his shoulder toward the up-lake end of the island. "There's a great tree over there—a pair of trees, really—to build a tree house in. I thought about it when I first came, last week, but I couldn't figure out how to get the materials over here in a canoe."

Before Megan could stop him, Sandy spoke out. "We've got a rowboat. I mean, it's our grandpa's, but he lets us use it when he's not fishing."

The boy ignored Megan, his gaze fixed on Sandy. "You willing to let me haul stuff in it?" Then, before Sandy could reply or Megan interrupt, he added, "You could help with it if you wanted."

"Sure," Sandy agreed. "Why not?"

Why not? Megan wondered angrily. Why should they? Although, if he'd been here since last week, maybe he had discovered the island before they had. Even so, she didn't want him here, not on an island she had considered her own.

"Where do you live?" Sandy was asking.

"The log cabin, over there."

"Your dad's the one who's writing a book?"

The boy's lip curled. "Yeah. That's all he does. He didn't use to be so grouchy, before he and my mom split up. I can't even talk around him, for fear he'll forget what he wants to write. I have to fix my own meals, because he doesn't remember to stop to eat."

"We're going to cook hot dogs today," Sandy offered. "You want some? We have enough, don't we, Megan?"

A sharp reply trembled on her tongue, and then she sighed. They couldn't run him off an island that didn't really belong to anybody. And they'd wanted to meet other kids, hadn't they?

It was clear she wasn't going to have the island to herself, no matter what she did. Well, if Sandy wanted this boy for a friend, she supposed he was entitled to that. She didn't think he was anyone *she* would want for a friend. Not like Annie. Every time she thought of Annie, she felt a painful tightness in her chest.

"Do what you want," she said ungraciously, and pushed past the pair of them, headed for the cave.

# eight

THE BOY'S NAME was Ben Jamison. His parents were divorced, and he had been living with his mother in Duluth, but now his mother was remarried and had just gone on a delayed honeymoon to Niagara Falls.

"I don't know why," Ben said. "They've been married for six months, and besides, she's seen Niagara Falls before."

"Are you going to live with your dad all the time now, or go back to Duluth when your mom comes home?"

They were crouched, the three of them, around the fire built just outside the cave. Megan, using a stick, poked at the hot dogs on the grill, rolling them over. The skins were beginning to blister, and the aroma made her mouth water. If it weren't for the stranger, she could have enjoyed

their first meal on the island, which she stubbornly continued to think of as *hers*.

Ben scratched at a mosquito bite on one bare ankle. "I
don't know. I don't think either one of them wants me."

Sandy gave him a shocked look, pausing in the act of
taking buns out of their plastic wrapper. "Your own parents
don't want you? Why not?"

"I guess I'm a nuisance," Ben said.

Sandy took out the buns and arranged them on the edge
of the grill to get warm. "How come?"

Ben thought about that so long that Megan, who had
been trying to ignore him, finally had to look at him. "I
get in trouble at school sometimes," he said at last. "And
they call Mom in for conferences. Lawrence says I've got
to shape up, because they don't have time to deal with
all my crap. Lawrence is her new husband."

"What kind of trouble?" Sandy wanted to know. "What
do you do?"

Ben shrugged. "Different things. I don't like school. I
don't like Lawrence. Sometimes . . ." Again he hesitated
to consider his reply. "Sometimes I don't even like Mom
very much. She's a lot more interested in Lawrence than
she is in me."

The hot dogs sizzled and split, dripping juice onto the
fire. Megan poked a stick into the nearest one, holding it
out toward the boys. "Get a bun for this," she instructed,
and Sandy took it and passed it along to their guest.

Sandy fixed his own hot dog with mustard and catsup
and chewed before he spoke again. "What about your dad,
then?"

Ben devoured half the hot dog and wiped mustard on
the back of his hand. "These are good. Well, I used to

want to go live with my dad, after he moved out and they filed for divorce. We got along great when we were all together. Only now he doesn't seem to like me much better than Lawrence does. He wants it quiet so he can write, and he was mad when I got here because he doesn't want anybody to bother him when he has a deadline. I guess Mom wrote him all about how big a pain I was, and I hardly got off the bus from Duluth before he was telling me I'd better not pull any of my crap—same word Lawrence used—on *him*, or he'd settle me down in a hurry."

Sandy's blue eyes were big and round. "You mean . . . beat you?"

Ben looked sheepish. "Oh, I don't think he'd do that. He never did before, anyway. But when he jumped me over some little thing, and I talked back—I was only trying to explain my side of it, see—he grabbed me and slammed me against the wall. It's easy to tell he doesn't want me here. I don't want to *be* here, either, but I got nowhere else to go." He finished off his hot dog and reached for another one.

"Gee," Sandy muttered. He gave Megan a look that said, He's as bad off as we are.

Megan wasn't in the mood to feel sorry for the boy, however. If he made everyone annoyed with him, what could he expect?

They ate in silence after that, finishing off the entire dozen wieners and buns, washing them down with canned pop. As soon as they'd finished, Ben was on his feet.

"Let's go look at that building site, OK? I think we could make a platform between those two trees—see the tall ones?—and then put up a roof over it. We could get it all closed in, so we could even sleep over here if we wanted to."

"I don't know if Grandpa will let us do that," Sandy said, but he was on his feet, too, following the leader.

Megan smothered her resentment and rose to bring up the rear. First Ben horned in on their island, and now he was making all the plans. Who made him the boss, anyway?

She could see why he would get on his parents' nerves. He didn't ask other people's opinions, assuming his own ideas were great. He acted as if he'd just been elected president.

Sandy didn't seem to mind. When Megan muttered her dissatisfaction while Ben was up in one of the trees for a closer look, Sandy was astonished.

"Well, he's got some good ideas, Megan! And he's got the lumber and tools to build a *real* tree house!"

"I was perfectly satisfied with the cave," Megan stated.

"Well, sure, I like it, too, but Ben's got some neat plans, Megan. And he's somebody to do things with while we're here."

Why did everything have to remind her that they were *here*, not at home, away from all their friends, uncertain about where they would go next, and when?

"See?" Ben called. "We could build a platform supported on these branches, between the two trees, and put a ladder up that trunk. We can use your boat, and get the stuff out of my dad's garage to start with."

"Will he let you use the lumber, too?"

"If it gets rid of me, he'll probably let me do anything," Ben said wryly. "Hey, the view up here is great! I can see to both ends of the lake, and there's something on that little bitty island over there we ought to investigate."

"That's my island, and I put a flag on it," Sandy told him. "Come on, Megan, let's climb up and see, too."

Megan declined, however. She had no desire to balance on a tree limb next to Ben Jamison. Still, unless she wanted to be left entirely alone, she was going to have to join the boys in whatever they decided to do.

In the end, they took both the canoe and the boat up the lake to the Jamisons' log cabin. They sorted out what they wanted of the tools from the garage, which looked as if it had been used to store junk for years; there was no room in it for the black Porsche parked in the yard.

"Hey, nice car," Sandy said.

"Yeah. Dad makes good money writing books. Only he got pretty upset over the divorce, I guess, and writing hasn't been so easy for him on this one. Here, take this saw. Megan, you take the nails and the hammer."

That was the way Ben was. Do this, do that. As if they were his servants.

Sandy didn't seem to mind. He was too impressed by the way Ben rattled off what they were going to do, and how. Megan smoldered, thinking up things to say to him when he gave her one order too many. Which was going to be very soon, she decided.

It took them two days to ferry the basic materials to the island. After that Ben began the actual building; he took it for granted that Megan and Sandy would run errands, hand things up to him, and in general wait on him.

Once, when he barked a demand for more nails, Megan tossed him the bag and said gruffly, "No wonder people think you're obnoxious. Did you ever hear of 'please' and 'thank-you?'"

To her surprise, Ben grinned. It made his face much more pleasant. "Yeah. Please get me those two-by-fours, and thank-you."

She didn't know what to say back, so she brought the

lumber from the pile on the ground. By the end of the second day of building, even Megan had to admit that the tree house was going to be better than the cave, which was open on the front and both sides except for some pine boughs.

The tree-house platform was big enough so they could spread out three sleeping bags if they wanted to. There was a window on each side, enabling them to see in all directions, though they had no glass for them. There was a shelf to keep food supplies on, and they even salvaged an old end table with a shelf under it for their dishes. They didn't have a way to cook, but Ben thought they would be just as well off using the grill at the mouth of the cave.

"It's not very far to walk, and it'll be safer than trying to have a stove in the hut. Especially when we don't have a stove," Ben announced.

"Oh, by all means, then," Megan said dryly, "let's do it that way if *you* think so."

Ben looked at Sandy. "What's the matter with her?"

Sandy shrugged. "You know how girls are."

Megan felt annoyance stirring again. Before she could think of a suitable comment, though, Ben asked, "Did your uncle find you?"

In the stillness a crow's cry sounded from the tall pines on the edge of the lake, and from far up the lake they heard an outboard motor, suggesting that new neighbors had arrived.

"Our uncle?" Sandy asked stupidly.

"Yeah," Ben said. "When my dad was in town this morning he said he met this guy asking about two redheaded kids in the general store. I hadn't told him about you until then—my dad, I mean—because he's been too busy to talk to me until he gets this difficult chapter written; but when he mentioned it, I figured it had to be you. There aren't that many redheads around, usually. The guy that runs the store didn't know you, but he suggested your uncle try asking at the post office."

Megan's mouth felt dry. "That's really strange. Because we don't have an uncle."

"No kidding? Well, I guess there must be some more redheads, then. Here, Sandy, grab the other end of this, and we'll get the roofing on. Then we won't have to worry that our stuff will get wet when it rains."

Sandy appeared to give the matter no further thought, but Megan's stomach was churning.

Who was the man who had claimed to be the "uncle" of two redheaded kids?

And if the man was really looking for Megan and Sandy, what did he want?

It wouldn't have frightened her if she hadn't known her mother was running away from something—or someone.

She didn't get a chance for a private conversation with Sandy until they got home, and Grandpa asked them to walk out to the main road and check the mailbox. "I need to keep an eye on supper so it won't scorch," he said. "Come right back, though, because this'll be ready in about twenty minutes."

As soon as they were out of earshot, Megan spoke. "I don't like the idea of some guy who says he's our uncle asking for us in town."

"We don't have an uncle, so he must be looking for somebody else," Sandy said, trotting to keep up with her.

"Or he's looking for us and he's lying about being our uncle because he thinks that will make people more willing to tell him where we are. We haven't been to town yet, so probably nobody knows we're here. But how many red-headed kids are there likely to be that the grocery man wouldn't know?"

"You think he really is looking for us?" Sandy had sobered. "What for?"

"Who knows? If he has to lie to find us, though, it's kind of suspicious, isn't it?"

"How would he know we're here? Unless Mom told him."

"If she told him, she'd have told him we were with Grandpa. And it didn't sound as if he mentioned our names, even. Just said he was looking for redheads. Our last name's not the same as Grandpa's, so probably the postmaster wouldn't know where we were, either. Not unless Grandpa told him we were coming, and he wasn't expecting us for another week or so."

Megan had to slow down because her furious pace had caused her to get a stitch in her side. "It makes me nervous, after the other things that have happened," she said.

"Are we going to tell Grandpa about it?"

"I don't know. Maybe. We'll think about it," Megan said uneasily.

They had reached the main road, and Sandy pulled open the door of the mailbox. "Two bills, and an ad for the general store in town, and . . . hey! You got a letter from Annie!"

Megan snatched the letter out of his hand. A letter from Annie! Annie hadn't been so mad at her that she refused to write back! She tore it open, but before she could empty the envelope, Sandy tugged at her arm.

"Come on, you can read it after we get home. It's too long to read in a minute or two, and I'm starved. Gramps said to come right home."

Megan hesitated, then folded the letter and put it into the pocket of her jeans. "OK. I want to read it slowly and enjoy it longer, anyway," she said.

It never occurred to her that the letter would leave her even more scared than she already was.

# nine

THERE WAS no opportunity to read Annie's letter until after the supper dishes had been washed and put away. Megan listened halfheartedly to the news on the radio, which was the usual sort of thing that didn't interest her very much: reports on a city council meeting, a governor's conference, a high speed police chase that ended in a crash, the death of some supposedly prominent person she'd never heard of.

Would it be on the radio if her mother got hurt or killed in a car crash?

It was a horrid thought—which just sprang into her mind—and Megan couldn't put it aside. What if something *did* happen to Karen Collier while she was away, and nobody even knew where to find her children or her father to tell them?

Megan put the last glass into the cupboard and headed for her tiny bedroom, glancing guiltily at the door when the letter crackled as she drew it out of her pocket. She wasn't quite sure why she felt guilty about writing to Annie, but she had an uncomfortable feeling that Grandpa might not approve.

She flopped across the bed and unfolded the pages, eager to see what her friend had to say.

*Dear Megan:*

*I was so glad to hear from you. It was very upsetting when you moved away without telling me. I knew your mother must have made you go, that it wasn't your fault, but I'm really disappointed that we won't be together at the lake.*

*I guess, from the postmark on your letter, that you did go to the cottage where your grandpa was staying. I'm addressing this in care of Mr. Davis, because you didn't give me a box number, so I hope it gets to you. Is it nice there? Have you been swimming, or is the water still too cold?*

*Mom let me get the swimsuit I wanted, the red and white one. I went to the pool with Shirley and Tammy, but it wasn't like going with you.*

*Mrs. Morgan told my mom you had moved out at night. We couldn't believe it, but Mrs. Morgan said she looked in the windows and you weren't there, only some boxes; and then that lady your mom worked with came and got them. She wouldn't tell Mrs. Morgan anything about where you were.*

*When I came home from school this afternoon, there was a man talking to Mr. Morgan on their front porch. After he went away, Mrs. Morgan came over and talked* to Mom and me. She said he was asking about you. I mean, your whole family, only he didn't seem sure what your name was. We all thought that was funny. He knew you were red-haired, though.

Well, I hope nothing is wrong. Mr. Morgan didn't know where you were, so he didn't tell the man anything like that. His nephew was there, you remember that homely one that yelled at the boys when Sandy hit a ball into their backyard? The one named Guy? My dad says he's 'the shifty one.' I guess he means Guy's a creep. He was asking questions, too, but Mom said it was nobody's business where you were, so she wouldn't have told even if she knew. She said you probably didn't have a chance to call me or anything, and it wasn't because we weren't friends anymore. I was sure glad to get your letter.

We've got one more day of school, and then we're out for the summer. Write to me again if you get this. I miss you.

Love, Annie.

There was a tight feeling in Megan's chest.

The Morgans had lived one house down from the Colliers, and though Mrs. Morgan was pleasant enough, she was awfully nosy. She always stopped Mom to talk and asked questions that Mom didn't usually answer, though she smiled and stayed polite. The idea of anybody getting information about the Colliers from the Morgans was disconcerting, and it made Megan feel as if she were guilty of something, even if she didn't have any idea of what it was.

It also made her scared. There had to be a reason why an unknown man would be looking for them. And since that happened right after the family had taken off without telling anyone, the two events seemed tied together. The timing was too perfect for it to be a coincidence.

If only Mom would come back and tell them what was wrong! She had to tell them, Megan thought fiercely. Whatever it was, surely she and Sandy would be better off knowing about it, rather than just getting more and more scared.

She smoothed out the pages and read them again, but it didn't make anything clearer. And the cold sense of dread grew in her stomach so that she felt half-sick with it.

"MEGAN! Wake up!"

The whisper was a hiss in the darkness, and she came awake groggily, rising on one elbow.

"Sandy? What's the matter?"

"Shhh! I don't want to wake Grandpa up. Listen, come into my bedroom and listen!"

What kind of a sentence was that? Megan wondered. "Listen to what?"

"If I knew what it was, I wouldn't have to ask you to listen to it, would I? I think somebody's prowling around outside."

She came wide awake then, aware of the night chill, or maybe it was goose bumps, because the fear came flooding back. After debating with herself for almost the entire evening, she'd finally shared Annie's letter with her brother. Then she'd wondered if that had been a mistake, because it was obvious that Sandy was scared, too.

And now he thought someone was prowling around the cottage.

Megan slid out of bed, shivering in her thin summer pajamas. Together they padded silently across the living room. Megan caught a little toe against the leg of a chair and stifled an exclamation of pain. Her heart was thudding so loudly it felt as if it could break out of her chest.

They reached the door of the bedroom where Sandy slept and eased inside. "Now listen!" Sandy commanded, so softly she could barely hear him.

At first there was nothing. Megan began to hope he had simply imagined whatever it was, or had had a bad dream. Sometimes when you woke from a nightmare, you couldn't tell what was real and what was not.

And then it came: from the porch outside Sandy's open window, the unmistakable sound of breathing. When she thought her heart would stop altogether, they heard a metallic sound, as if someone had run into the trash can and shoved it against the wall.

Sandy's hand reached for hers, and they stood there, not daring to speak. If they could hear whoever was out there, *he* could also hear *them*.

Why hadn't she told Grandpa about the stranger in town, asking for redheaded kids? Why hadn't she showed him Annie's letter? Why wasn't her mom here where she belonged, so they didn't have to try to deal with this themselves?

The metallic scraping sound came again, and then there was a clatter, a scrabbling noise, and a crash.

A moment later, while they were still paralyzed with fright, Grandpa spoke behind them. "What in tarnation's going on?"

He didn't wait for an answer but clumped noisily through to the kitchen, opened the back door, and looked out. Megan and Sandy were right behind him when he turned on the light.

"Well, fella, where did you come from?" Grandpa asked.

He didn't sound scared, so Megan eased up to look past him.

Tension began to ooze out of her, making her aware of how shaky she felt.

There was an intruder on the porch all right, but it wasn't the stranger from town or back home. It was a dog that had just knocked over the garbage can and clawed the lid off from it to rummage through the pork chop bones from supper.

He was big and brownish-gray in the light from the dim bulb. He lifted a huge head to look at them, poised to run, until Grandpa spoke.

"Hungry, are you? Where'd you come from, boy? The way your ribs are sticking out, I'd say it's been a few days since you've had much to eat."

The dog continued to hesitate, wary yet unwilling to be driven off.

Sandy was tremulous in his relief. "He's starving, Grandpa. Can we give him something to eat?"

"Well, he could have picked a better time to get acquainted than two o'clock in the morning," Grandpa said. "But he's hungry, all right. See if he's interested in those leftover pancakes I was going to feed the chipmunks tomorrow."

The pancakes vanished in three gulps when Sandy tossed them to the dog. The animal then gave a couple of tentative wags of his tail, obviously looking for more.

"There was a little of that cream gravy left," Megan offered. "And a few peas."

"All right. Pour those over some bread, that's the best we can do on the spur of the moment," Grandpa agreed.

For the next ten minutes, they rounded up every scrap that wasn't enough for another meal, and the dog ate every morsel. By the time they came to the end of it, he was licking crumbs off Sandy's hand.

"Can we keep him?" Sandy demanded.

Grandpa ran a hand through the gray hair that was standing up in tufts, making it look even worse. "That's no decision to make in the middle of the night. Remember, once this cast comes off I have to go back to work, and I don't have a place in the city for a big dog."

"Maybe Mom would let us keep him," Sandy said eagerly.

"And maybe she won't, if you all wind up in an apartment," Grandpa said dryly. "But I guess it won't hurt to let him hang around until morning, anyway."

"We could use a good watchdog," Sandy said. "Couldn't we, Megan?"

Now was the time, maybe, to tell Grandpa about the stranger who had asked about redheaded kids. Somehow, though, Megan's tongue wouldn't quite say the words, and then it was too late, at least for now. Grandpa slid the bolt on the back door, hitched up his pajamas, and headed back to bed. "We'll talk about it tomorrow," he said. "Good night again."

Back in her own bed, Megan took a while to warm up. Grandpa had left the dog out on the porch, but after Grandpa's snores drifted through the cottage, there were other sounds. Surreptitious ones that Megan figured out without getting alarmed again.

Sandy was bringing the dog in through the window, and she had no doubt that *he* was getting warm faster because the dog had joined him on the single bed.

Tomorrow, she thought, she'd better tell Grandpa what

they knew, and what they suspected. Just in case anyone really did come prowling around.

It was a long time before she stopped straining to hear sounds in the surrounding darkness and fell asleep.

## *ten*

"GOING TO BE hot today," Grandpa said cheerfully the following morning when Megan came into the kitchen, still buttoning her shirt. "Ought to warm up that lake water pretty fast if it stays like this."

The sun flooded through the kitchen windows, and there was the delicious aroma of bacon and toast; as she took her place at the table, Grandpa slid a plate of eggs toward her. "Eat up. You kids are on your own for lunch, all right? I have to drive into the city to have this foot X-rayed, make sure it's healing the way it's supposed to. While I'm at it, I'll do some shopping. The way this country air is increasing your appetites, I'm having trouble keeping enough groceries on hand, and they'll cost less in the city than they do here in the village."

Grandpa had already eaten. So had Sandy, apparently,

because he was sitting on the back steps feeding the dog. In daylight the animal looked just as large as Megan remembered, and even homelier.

Grandpa gave her a pat on the shoulder. "If you go out on the water, don't forget your life jackets," he said. "See you around suppertime."

There was no opportunity to tell him about the mysterious man who had been asking about them, nor about Annie's letter. He went down the steps past Sandy and the dog, and got in the car and drove away.

Megan carried her plate out to join her brother, lifting it out of reach when the dog would have finished it off for her. "Down! Sit!" she commanded, and was pleased when the dog obediently thumped his rear end on the porch and looked up expectantly.

"He's been trained," Sandy pointed out. "He did what you wanted. Now you have to give him something."

"Why? He's supposed to mind whether you feed him or not," Megan said, but she dropped him a bit of toast. "What kind of dog is he, anyway? I don't think I ever saw one that was uglier."

"Grandpa said mostly Russian wolfhound, but probably three or four other breeds besides." Sandy ran a hand over the big head, and was licked on the ear in return. "I'm going to call him Wolf."

"Why? He doesn't look much like a wolf." Megan cleaned her plate, wishing the dog weren't drooling as he watched her every bite. "He looks more like a tramp."

"I always wanted a dog I could call Wolf," Sandy asserted. "This is as close as I'll ever get, so he's Wolf."

"You're not going to be able to keep him," Megan warned. "There's no way Mom's going to let you. We might wind up in an apartment where they won't let you have pets, or in the city where there's no place for him to run. And a dog that size has to be expensive to feed. You want to eat tuna-fish casseroles *every* day instead of twice a week?"

"I'll earn the money to feed him," Sandy said. "I'll get a paper route or something. I like him, Megan. Are you trying to spoil everything for me?"

"No." She stooped to lower the plate so Wolf could lick off the crumbs and the hardening egg yolk. "I'm just trying to be realistic. If we're running away all the time, Mom isn't going to let us drag a dog along. Especially one that looks like this one. Everybody who sees him will remember him."

"The way they know we have red hair," Sandy observed. "Who is it, Megan? What do they want with us?"

"I don't know." A frown etched itself into her face, as a new thought came to her. "It's like . . . well, if some guy is asking about redheads, it's you and me he's looking for. Not Mom. And *we* didn't do anything."

"It's crazy," Sandy said, and she had to agree with him.

"Hey! You guys got the boat today? I got a bunch of stuff to take over to the island!"

Ben came walking up from the beach, stopping at the foot of the steps. "Where'd you get the ugly mutt?"

"He's a stray, I guess. I'm going to keep him, at least for now. I'm calling him Wolf."

"I'd call him Mutt," Ben said, but he reached down a hand to stroke the brindled muzzle, and Wolf licked his hand. "I always wanted a dog. My mom wouldn't let me have one."

"Your dad has a dog, doesn't he? We've seen him throwing sticks for it on the beach." Megan retrieved the licked-clean plate and hesitated before returning it to the kitchen.

"Missy. Yeah. She's a purebred Irish setter. I guess he

got her to keep him company after he wasn't part of the family anymore. She's OK, but she's *his* dog, not mine, and she's not used to kids. All she wants to do is chase sticks. When I talk to her, tell her to do anything, she looks as me as if I'm speaking Swahili."

"What's that?" Sandy wanted to know.

"A language they speak in Africa. Hey, can we use the boat? I want to haul a bunch of groceries over there, so we can have whole meals. I may even stay there tonight."

"Alone?" Sandy asked.

"Unless you want to come along." Ben spoke as if it didn't matter, one way or the other. Megan remembered how frightened she had been last night, when they'd thought there was a prowler on the porch; would she be afraid to be out on the island at night? But why should she be? It would probably be safer than staying here, if that stranger came looking for them.

What did he want? If he was the one they kept running away from, her mom must think he was dangerous, but why would he want to harm a couple of kids who didn't even know him?

Ben was staring at her. "Is something wrong? Can't we take the boat today?"

Megan moistened her lips. "It's not the boat. Grandpa went to the city to have X-rays done and to shop, so he won't be here to use it. It's . . ." She hesitated, and then the words burst out as if she could no longer hold them. "Did your dad say what that guy looked like, the one who claimed to be our uncle, that was asking about us?"

"No, just said a guy. You want me to ask him what the man looked like? When he's not writing, I mean. When he is, I don't interrupt him unless the house is on fire, or something like that. He's OK when he isn't trying to finish a book by a deadline, but right now . . ." Ben shrugged expressively. "What's the deal? Who do you think this guy is?"

"Well, he isn't our uncle, because we don't have one." She knew, quite suddenly, that even if she didn't like Ben all that well, even if he was bossy and acted as if they were his servants, she was going to tell him everything. Sandy was too young to help very much, but maybe Ben with his know-it-all attitude could figure out more than she'd been able to do.

They stood there in the warm morning sunshine while she told him. She brought out the letter from Annie and showed him that, too. Her heart was pounding as she waited for his reaction to it.

Ben read without speaking, then handed the letter back. "What do you think's going on?"

"We don't know, only it's scary," Megan said.

"You don't want him to find you? Maybe you've inherited a million dollars or something, and that's why he's asking about you."

Sandy's face lit up. "It could be something like that, Megan!"

"Oh, sure. That's why Mom keeps moving us around so he can't find us. She knows, and she doesn't want us to be able to afford a roast more than once a month," Megan said. She'd intended to sound sarcastic, but all she did was sound scared.

"How long's she been doing that?" Ben wanted to know. "Moving around a lot?"

Sandy and Megan exchanged glances. "As long as we can remember, I guess. Since we were little kids, anyway."

"And you don't have any clues why." Ben was thoughtful, and to Megan's chagrin he picked up at once on the thing that had taken her much longer to recognize. "Well, it sounds like it's you kids this guy is looking for, not your mom, so it can't be for anything *she* did."

Sandy was indignant. "*We* didn't do anything, either!"

"Certainly not when we were practically babies," Megan added.

"There's one sure way to find out," Ben stated. "Talk to the guy and ask him what he wants with you."

The idea hit Megan like a blow to the chest. "But what if he . . . if he's dangerous?"

"Besides, we don't know who he is," Sandy pointed out. "And we don't know where."

"If he's looking for you around here, he's probably still in town. There aren't many places to stay . . . one motel, one rooming house, from what Dad said. He looked at them before he rented the log cabin we're in now. You want me to tell my dad about this, ask him to help us, when I can catch him willing to listen for a few minutes?"

Megan hesitated. She didn't know Mr. Jamison, and after what Ben had said she wasn't sure they could expect much help from him. If he wasn't supportive of his own son, if he made Ben feel unwanted, how likely was he to respond to the needs of a couple of kids he didn't even know?

"Not yet," she decided finally. "I'll tell Grandpa when he comes home."

It didn't make her feel any better to have made up her mind to do that. She was glad Ben knew, though, so it wasn't just she and Sandy keeping an eye out for the mysterious stranger, although how much good another kid could do she didn't know.

"If we can use the boat," Ben said, "let's get going. I've got a whole pile of stuff on the beach in front of our cabin to haul over to the island." He was off at a trot, Sandy and Wolf right behind him. Megan stared after them.

So much for feeling better because someone else knew as much as she did. All they could think of was playing around. She wished desperately that she'd showed Annie's letter to Grandpa last night; he would have put down his book and listened to her, she knew he would have. And maybe if he'd known about the man asking after them in the village, he wouldn't have gone away and left them here alone for the day.

Ordinarily the prospect of being on their own from breakfast to suppertime would have been great. Now the day stretched ahead of her, endless hours of it, when there would be no adult around in case anything bad happened. The fear was like icy teeth, gnawing at Megan's stomach.

The boys had shoved the boat almost free of the beach. Sandy jumped in, and they were both laughing as Wolf, afraid of being left behind, scrambled wildly after him, nearly overturning the boat, which Ben was holding for Megan.

"Come on, hurry up, before that idiot of a dog swamps us and we have to bail," Ben called. "Maybe you'd better leave him here," he added to Sandy, as Wolf rocked the boat again in his frantic effort to reach the bow where Sandy was seated. "I don't want to dump a load of groceries in the lake."

"Sit, Wolf! Sit!" Sandy commanded. "Wait a minute, Ben. If I can get him to stay in one place, he'll be all right! We can't leave him here, he'd probably try to swim after us, and he might not be able to swim as far as the island."

Megan rolled up her pant legs and stepped in, wishing she could feel as carefree as the boys. The sound of an engine brought her head around so quickly that she rocked the boat, though it was in no danger of capsizing. A sleek black car showed through the trees, and for a moment panic overwhelmed her, until she realized that it was going out, toward the main road, rather than coming in.

Ben looked, too. "My dad. He said he was having trouble with his typewriter. He's been grumbling about it, and he said if it got any worse he'd have to take it to the city to get it fixed. Boy, I hope they've got a loaner, or they can fix it right away, so he can go on working, or he'll be miserable to live with." Ben took a few steps, soaking the legs of his jeans, and hopped into the boat as he shoved it off. "I'll row," he said, as if the decision were his to make.

Megan didn't care about that. Let him make his muscles ache and get slivers in his hands from the old oars. She was thinking about Mr. Jamison going to town. That left the three of them—Sandy, Ben, and herself—completely unprotected here at the lake.

Megan had taken the seat at the stern, facing Ben as he rowed. Wolf had settled down, holding still with Sandy's hand on his collar, and they were about twenty yards from shore when Ben looked directly at Megan, and she saw that he hadn't put their situation out of mind, after all.

"You know what you did when you wrote to your friend Annie, don't you?" he asked.

"What do you mean?" Megan demanded. Even before he replied, though, her heart had taken on that almost painfully rapid beat. The uneasiness she had been feeling ever since she had put the letter to Annie in the mailbox suddenly congealed in a great guilty lump in her chest. Because she *did* know, even if she hadn't put it into words, even in her own mind. Because she didn't want to be the one responsible for making a bad situation worse.

"You told them where you are. Back there where you used to live."

The rapid beating in her chest became a thunderous clamor. Megan's fingers curled over the edges of the seat, gripping it so tightly that her knuckles turned white. "Annie won't tell, if that man comes back."

"No? Not even if he convinces her he's your uncle?" Ben persisted, dealing more expertly with the oars, sending the boat skimming over the surface of the water. "Besides, she's probably not the only one who saw *your* letter. Saw the postmark. If they track you as far as Lakewood, they'll find you here. The mail carrier delivered the letter from Annie to your grandpa's mailbox, so that means the next time anybody asks in the village, the postmaster will probably tell them where you are."

Megan swallowed, almost hating him for having said it, yet knowing it was true, that somehow she'd given away the place Mom had hidden them. To keep them safe, that was what she'd said: They'd be safe here.

She wanted to cry, but with Ben watching her she was determined not to. "I'll tell Grandpa, as soon as he comes home," she said.

She hoped that wouldn't be too late.

# *eleven*

WOLF WAS in and out of the boat several times while they were loading it in front of the log cabin. He left wet footprints on everything, shook himself dry over their supplies, and generally made a nuisance of himself in his eagerness to be as close to his new friends and benefactors as possible.

Ben grew impatient. "He's making a mess of my blankets. Make him get out, Sandy, before he eats any more of that cheese. He already got the bologna. There isn't room for him in the boat, anyway, if we take this last box."

Reluctantly, Sandy ordered the dog out of the boat, and the others climbed in and pushed off for the trip to the island. Wolf, however, was very unhappy to be left behind.

He ran along the shore, barking and whining. When Sandy ordered him to stay, and then to sit, Wolf ignored the commands, simply driven to further frenzy by the sound of the boy's voice.

"We'll bring him on the next trip," Ben offered, but then he muttered a curse under his breath.

"What's the matter?" Megan swiveled all the way around so she could see, and there was Wolf, striking out after them, swimming.

"We gotta go back," Sandy said after a moment. "He can't swim all that distance. He'll drown."

"He can probably swim it," Ben said, though since he didn't sound completely confident of that, Sandy was not reassured.

"What if he doesn't? We can't haul him into the boat out here, even if we wait for him. We have to go back, Ben."

Ben scowled. "And do what? Is somebody going to stay on shore with him? We still don't have room for him!"

"Well, maybe Megan could stay with him, unless she'd rather unload the boat and haul the supplies up to the tree house," Sandy suggested. "There's a lot of heavy stuff, though, this trip."

Megan stared back, swallowing hard, watching the dog's dark head as he came toward them, seeing the empty beach behind him. There was no one at home, either at the Jamisons' or Grandpa's. She'd never thought of herself as a scaredy-cat, but she was afraid now of being left behind by the boys.

Still, it was clear that that fool dog was going to drown trying to keep up with them unless someone stayed with him. And if she didn't do it, it would have to be Sandy.

She swallowed again. "OK. Put it into shore in front of our place. I'll stay. Only come and get us as soon as you've unloaded, all right?"

Ben obligingly lifted one oar out of the water and pulled deeply with the other to turn the boat. Wolf immediately turned to follow the new course, and he was in the shallow water by the time Megan jumped out and waded ashore. He shook all over her, ecstatic that someone had returned to keep him company.

"Come on, stupid," she told him. "We might as well go out and see if the mailman's come yet. There might be a letter from Mom."

Anything, she thought, was better than sitting and waiting for the boys to come back for her.

Wolf was perfectly happy now that he hadn't been abandoned. He frolicked around her, licking her hands when he got close enough, his tongue lolling out. He looked silly, this huge beast acting as if he were a puppy, but Megan couldn't quite be amused.

She got annoyed with Ben and his know-it-all ways, but in this case she had to admit, at least to herself, that he was right. She hadn't thought out the business of letting Annie know where she was. If the stranger thought they were here, it could be because of that letter to Annie.

The reason her mom hadn't let her call and tell Annie where they were going, Megan realized belatedly, was that she wanted to prevent just this kind of thing from happening. If no one knew where they were, no one could tell anyone else who came snooping around. And Mom had known there would probably be someone asking questions.

If only she would come home! If only she would explain!

She walked through the silent woods, along the dirt road that led out to the paved main road. It was warm and peaceful; small birds twittered in the surrounding trees, and it should have been a pleasant walk. Yet Megan couldn't forget that something frightening was going on, and that she was all by herself.

Wolf took off after a squirrel, barking ferociously, then returned panting when the small creature scurried up a tree out of reach.

How easily the squirrel had escaped an enemy! It wasn't so easy for people, especially when they didn't even know who the enemy was, or why they were an enemy.

She heard a car coming along the main road. Megan stopped, staring through the remaining trees, every nerve tightening as the approaching car slowed down.

It was white, with a wine-red roof. She could see it clearly through the fringe of birches between two towering pines. And it was stopping at the row of mailboxes.

She felt as if the blood grew thick in her veins, as if she were suddenly unable to breathe, or move. Wolf was now pursuing a tiny yellow butterfly, with no more success than he'd had catching the squirrel. Megan didn't look after him; she was watching the car.

The driver was a man, though she couldn't make out what he looked like, only that he wore a pale blue shirt. He turned and glanced back over his shoulder as he began to back the car down the road.

To turn around, or to drive on this road that led around the edge of the lake?

Megan took several quick steps off the dirt road and dropped to her stomach amidst the ferns as soon as the driver of the white car nosed his vehicle onto the side road.

She lay flat, her cheek pressed against a few twigs atop the mossy ground. Her heart was making so much noise she scarcely heard the car engine until it had passed her. Then she lifted her head enough to peer cautiously over a fallen log.

The car headed toward the lake, then swung to the left, out of her sight. Where was it going? As far as she knew, there was no one living on this road except the Jamisons and Grandpa Davis. Which did he want? Neither of them had names on their mailboxes, because they were only renters for the summer.

When the sound of the motor died away, Megan dared to get to her feet. Wolf came galloping up, nudging her with a wet nose.

"If you give me away, I'm going to wish I'd let you drown," she told him in a stern whisper. "Come on, and be quiet. I want to know where he went."

She walked quickly, all senses heightened by the apprehension that had washed over her the moment the car came into view. Maybe it was only someone wanting to look at the rental cottages farther up the lake. Or someone for Mr. Jamison. Please, please, she prayed, let it not be the stranger.

The dog seemed to sense that something was wrong. He whined and licked her hand, and she brushed her fingertips lightly over the big head.

"Be quiet," she told him, and hoped he'd mind her better than he had when they'd tried to leave him on the beach.

The car had driven into Grandpa's yard.

Megan stood well back in the trees, seeing that the man had gotten out and walked up onto the porch to knock. His back was toward her, but she dropped low anyway, in case he turned around.

He wore navy slacks with the light blue shirt. He had

dark hair, and a gold watch glinted on his wrist where the sun struck it.

On her knees, Megan crept forward until she could see the Illinois license plate on the car. She had nothing to write with; could she memorize the number?

Miraculously, Wolf was behaving. He, too, had dropped to his belly, and when she carefully parted a clump of ferns to move closer still to the stranger's car, Wolf moved with her.

The man on the porch knocked once more, then swore audibly and came down the steps again. For a few seconds he seemed to be staring directly at her. Megan's breathing stopped until she realized that looking from bright sunlight into the shadows must have kept him from seeing her. She was thankful she'd worn an old brown shirt today; almost anything else would have stood out from the surrounding forest.

The man walked toward his car, hesitated, then went on toward the lake. He paused to look down at the sand, and Megan knew what there was to see. Footprints, and the marks where the boat had been drawn up above the water.

He studied them for a few minutes, while Megan crouched with one restraining hand on Wolf's massive head to keep him quiet. She was glad of his warm presence, and she wondered if he would try to protect her if the man discovered her.

She was near enough now to see that the license was not from a government agency; she knew they had special plates. It wasn't a police car. Besides, if it had been a policeman asking about redheaded kids, either back home or here in Lakewood, he would have identified himself, the way they always did on TV.

The man turned again, facing her, and once more Megan froze. He was younger than Grandpa, maybe the age of Annie's father, she thought. He had thick black eyebrows and a wide mouth that twisted in what appeared to be annoyance.

For what must have been ten minutes, Megan hid in the woods, low on the ground, watching the man prowl around Grandpa's cottage. He tried the door, which was locked during the daytime for the first time since they'd been there; that was because Grandpa would be away all day, and the kids had intended to be out on the island. If the intruder had known it, the key was hidden under the top layer of rocks in a tin can at the edge of the porch.

Megan didn't know if eleven-year-old kids ever had heart attacks, but her chest really hurt when she kept holding her breath. What if she'd left Sandy here with the dog, instead of staying herself? Would Sandy have had the sense to stay out of sight, or would he have barged over and asked who the man was?

That had been Ben's idea: find the man and ask him what he wanted. Ben had a big mouth. She wondered if he'd be brave enough to do it, himself, if he were the one involved.

Now the stranger was peering in the kitchen windows. After a moment, he went on around the porch, where he was probably looking in the living-room windows.

Though there was nothing inside that Megan knew of that could incriminate them, there were signs of the rooms being occupied. Had she and Sandy left anything in plain sight that would indicate they were redheaded, and kids? She couldn't remember. She could only wait. The man came back around the corner on the porch, his hands jammed into his pants pockets, frowning. He tried the door again, and when he hesitated Megan wondered desperately if he were going to break in. He would certainly be able to tell, if he did, that there were two kids living there, as well as Grandpa.

And then something happened that made her literally break out in a cold sweat.

As he started down the steps, his foot struck the can of rocks that served both as a doorstop when they wanted to prop the screen open to carry in groceries, and as a repository for the key.

The can was on the edge of the porch. It went over, spilling its contents down the steps and into the yard.

Megan stared in horror as he kicked impatiently at the can, sending it across the yard. Was the key lying in plain sight, in front of him?

He hesitated, then retrieved the can and began to scoop up rocks to put back into it. So nobody would know he'd been there, she thought. Oh, please, please, don't let him find the key so he can get into the house!

He put the can back in place on the porch, then walked to his car and drove away.

Megan stayed on her knees for a long time after the sound of the motor had died away, after her heart rate had returned to normal, feeling the cold sweat dry on her body in the warm summer breeze. Then finally she got up and went out into the open.

He had missed the key because it had fallen beside the steps rather than on them. She picked it up with trembling fingers, not daring to put it back in the same place. Instead, she slipped it into the pocket of her jeans.

The sun felt good, but she was still icy on the inside.

Who was the man, and what did he want?

# twelve

MEGAN SAT on the porch, staring out across the lake. There was no sign of the boat, or the boys. Nothing stirred on the island. Not even a bird sang, now. The only thing she heard was Wolf's panting beside her.

She didn't know how much time had passed since Ben and Sandy had left her behind. They *had* taken a heavy load, and carrying all those things up the steep rock slope, and up the island to the tree house, would take time. Still, they would surely be starting for shore before long.

Wolf suddenly lifted his big head, listening.

Megan's heart leaped. "What is it?" she whispered.

The dog was definitely alert, hearing something she could not yet hear. She strained to detect it, too, and then, as Wolf rose to his feet, looking toward the road, Megan slid off the porch and stood up, too.

"What is it?" she whispered again.

Wolf looked at her, tentatively wagging his tail, remaining alert.

He'd only been here since last night, she remembered. Would he feel protective of this place—of her—when he was not yet securely a member of the family?

He'd sensed her fear a short time ago, though, she thought hopefully. He'd stayed quiet beside her when she was hiding in the woods. He hadn't betrayed her whereabouts while the man in the white car was here. He hadn't bounded out to make friends, though he hadn't growled, either.

"Is he coming back?" she wondered aloud.

And then she heard it, too.

A car was coming. Grandpa, returning early? Or Mr. Jamison in his sleek black Porsche? She'd never met Ben's father, but if it was him she was going to run out and flag him down, tell him she was frightened, and why.

No sooner had she thought that than the car stopped, still out of sight, and she knew positively it wasn't the Porsche. *That* had purred smoothly and quietly, and this car didn't. This one sounded as if it needed a tune-up.

And it had stopped somewhere between the cottage and the road. There were no other houses and no other driveways, and if the car had gone past the end of Grandpa's driveway, she'd have seen it, as they'd seen Ben's father leaving earlier.

Why had Grandpa picked today to leave them alone and go to town? What would happen when the man came back, even if she could warn Grandpa first?

Would he dare go to the police? If calling in the authorities were an option, surely Mom would have done it before this. So what other choice was there?

For the first time Megan began to understand why her mother had gathered them up and run away. She fought the impulse herself to run blindly, with no refuge in mind . . . simply to get away from the man who menaced her family in some way she didn't understand.

There was no time to lose. The car she had heard might be someone no more dangerous than the mail carrier, but she couldn't take the chance.

Megan ran toward the beach, reaching for the life jacket hanging on the tree and putting it on with fingers so cold and clumsy they could scarcely cope with the fasteners. Then she shoved the canoe into the water. If the man came back, or someone else came, she wouldn't be there.

BEN AND SANDY met her at the beach on the island. They were getting ready to push off in the boat when Megan rounded the rock that formed one arm of the little cove.

They stared at her wet clothes and dripping hair as she nosed the canoe toward shore.

"What happened to you?" Sandy demanded.

At the sound of Sandy's voice, Wolf leaped to his feet from where he had been sitting in the canoe, eager to reach his new young master. The canoe slid in alongside the rowboat, and the big dog tried to leap from one to the other.

The result was that Wolf overturned the canoe, landing both himself and Megan in the lake.

They were on the rocky shelf, so the water wasn't very deep. Wolf swam ashore and shook himself, sending a shower over Megan as she rose to the surface, spluttering, and waded past a laughing Ben.

"Looks like he's even more dangerous in a canoe than in a boat. Why didn't you leave him on the mainland?"

"Because," Megan said, drawing a deep breath, "he wouldn't stay there. That's how I got wet the first time. He swam after me and tried to climb in with me." She twisted at her hair, wringing out some of the water. "Besides, I didn't have the heart to leave him, after he stood by me when that man came and I had to hide in the woods."

Ben's amusement died abruptly. "What man? What happened?"

She told them, quickly, concisely. She didn't admit how scared she'd been—how scared she still was—but she could tell they knew. It was in their faces; they were scared, too.

"A guy with Illinois plates," Ben mused when she had finished. "Are you sure he wasn't a cop?"

"I suppose he could have been, but he didn't act like one." She waited defensively for him to ask why she hadn't demanded of the man who he was and what he wanted.

He didn't. "Wonder what he'd have done," he muttered, "if he'd found you there."

Sandy's blue eyes were enormous. "Do you think he'll come back?"

"I'd bet on it," Ben said impatiently. "If he came all the way from Illinois, and asked questions about you back home and then here in Lakewood, and came out here to the lake, he isn't going to give up and go away just because nobody was home this morning."

Sandy licked his lips. "Do you think he's . . . dangerous?"

Megan felt the man was dangerous. She had been terrified, crouching there in the woods while the stranger prowled around the cottage, testing doors and windows. She was nevertheless annoyed when Ben said, before she could speak, "Of course." The response sounded as if he meant to add "stupid" on the end of it.

Ben considered the situation. "Your grandpa probably will be gone until suppertime. And no telling how long Dad will be away, maybe that long, too. I guess there's only one thing to do."

"What?" Sandy asked, his voice squeaking.

"Stay here. I've got binoculars, we can take turns watching and see what he does if he comes back. Unless he goes down to our place and swipes our canoe, there's no way he can get at us here on the island," Ben said. "Come on, let's go back to the tree house where we can see your cottage."

He led the way up over the rock, with Sandy and Megan following. For once Megan didn't resent the way Ben took charge without asking anyone else's opinion.

For a few hours, until one of the grown-ups came home, they ought to be safe here on the island, she thought. Megan wished the idea made her feel better than it did.

"MAKE ME another sandwich. Boiled ham with mayonnaise," Ben said. He was lying flat on his stomach on the deck that projected from the side of the tree house, so that he could rest on his elbows as he held the binoculars to his eyes. The binoculars were at the moment trained on Grandpa Davis's cottage, although from time to time he swept them along the rest of the shore to make sure he wasn't missing any action.

He'd already had two sandwiches, and Sandy had had one. Megan felt too much tension to be hungry, though several hours had passed and nothing more had happened. Whoever had driven the car that needed a tune-up off the main road had never appeared where the trio on the island could see him. Maybe that should have made her feel better, but Megan only felt more tense than ever, waiting. Knowing the man would eventually return.

"Put a slice of cheese on it, too," Ben added.

When she didn't move from where she sat cross-legged in the doorway of the house, Ben lowered the glasses to twist his head in her direction.

"What's the matter? We can't be out of cheese yet. I brought enough food out here to last for a week."

"Who was your servant this time last year?" Megan asked, disgruntled.

Ben's grin was disarming. "I think it was my friend Fred. Yes, it was definitely Fred. But Fred's in Duluth. Besides, he's not allowed to associate with me anymore."

"Why not?" Sandy asked, intrigued. He was sprawled inside the hut on a sleeping bag, reading a comic book. Ben had thought of practically everything.

"His folks said I talked him into skipping school to go swimming. Actually he was the one who said he wanted to swim because it was so hot, and we didn't have anything left of school but study hall and P.E. We didn't think anybody would miss us. Besides, how did I know Fred would lose our bus fare so we'd have to walk all the way home and we'd be so late both our dads would call the cops to look for us? Well, Lawrence is only my stepfather, and I don't think he was worried as much as mad. Lawrence must never have been a kid. He has no sense of humor whatsoever."

"Did Fred make you sandwiches?" Sandy asked, tossing aside the comic book.

"Fred did everything I wanted him to do," Ben said, nodding. "Until they grounded him."

"Why?" Megan asked.

"I just told you why. We skipped the last two periods. . . ."

"No, I mean why did Fred wait on you?"

"He liked me. He looked up to me. He felt worthwhile, waiting on me. It gave him something to do besides count his zits."

"I'm not Fred," Megan said. "I don't like waiting on anybody. Especially when they don't say . . ."

"Please!" both boys chorused. "And thank-you!"

"Make your own . . ." Megan began, and then broke off, suddenly breathing more quickly.

"What's the matter?" Ben grabbed for the binoculars and swiveled them toward the cottage. "They're back! Or somebody is. Medium-blue Ford Escort, I think. Not a white car with a red top, so it's somebody different."

There were any number of reasons why someone might legitimately drive into the yard. A meter reader, a delivery person, someone who was lost and wanted directions to a local cabin on the lake. Why, then, was Megan's mouth so dry? "Let me see," she requested.

Ben handed over the glasses as the car doors opened and two men got out. "Is one of them the guy you saw before?"

The two figures seemed to leap toward her through the powerful lenses; she focused first on one, then the other. "No. These are different men. They're younger." There was a tremor in her voice as she returned the binoculars.

"Let me see, too," Sandy said, and Ben handed them over to him. He studied the men in silence for a moment, then frowned as he lowered the glasses. "I think I've seen one of them before, maybe. The smallest guy, the one with dark hair."

"Where?" Ben asked.

"I don't know. I can't remember."

"Fat lot of help you are," Ben observed, so that Megan bristled.

"He can't help it if he can't remember," she said in a challenging tone.

Ben refused to be riled. "You're no help, either. Get this description: the first one is skinny, dark haired. The second one is a lot bigger, blond, and he's wearing glasses with dark rims. They're both wearing jeans, I think, and plaid shirts."

Sandy had reached for a pencil and a pad—Ben really had thought of everything, though it was doubtful those had been provided for such a purpose—and scribbled some notes. "What are we keeping this information for? Are we going to call the police? What if that first one *was* the police?"

"Then they ought to congratulate us on being observant." Ben swung the glasses slightly. "I think that's a Minnesota license plate."

Again the binoculars were handed back and forth. Although the glasses were powerful ones—Megan suspected they were expensive and Mr. Jamison probably would be upset when he found out where they were—it was enough of a distance across the water to make it hard to be sure about the license. "It could be Minnesota colors," she said finally.

"What's that prove?" Sandy asked.

"Nothing. No more than the Illinois ones prove. Write it down anyway. It's evidence," Ben said. "Who do you know in Illinois?"

"Nobody," Megan and Sandy answered together.

Even without the aid of the binoculars, Megan could see that the two men were poking around the cottage, the same as the first man had done. They didn't walk down to the water's edge, though. After a few minutes, they got into the blue car and drove away.

Ben set aside the binoculars. "It makes your eyes tired to look so hard. Have you thought of who the smaller guy might be, Sandy? Or where you saw him?"

"It had to have been at home," Sandy said. "That's the only place I've been in a year, until we came up here. I can't remember who he is, though. What are we going to do now?"

Once more it was Ben who made the decision. "Stay here, until either my dad or your grandpa comes home."

He sat up and went through a carton of supplies until he came to a package of doughnuts. He opened them, took out one with chocolate frosting, and extended the box. "Have some. They're great."

Sandy took one with coconut frosting, and after a moment's hesitation, Megan selected maple topping. It had been a long time since breakfast, and Wolf had eaten part of that.

She stretched to see the dog, lying at the foot of the tree below the platform. Immediately he lifted his head and whined, wagging his tail.

She broke off a chunk of the doughnut and dropped it down to him, where he gobbled it quickly, and waited expectantly for more. She felt funny feeding him Ben's groceries, however, so she drew back far enough so the dog couldn't see her.

For the rest of the afternoon they stayed hidden in the

tree house, taking turns watching the shore, but nothing stirred in the clearing around the cottage.

"WHAT IF nobody comes home?" Sandy asked. "What if we have to stay here all night?"

"We've got sleeping bags and food," Ben said. "We've even got the lantern, but I guess we'd better not light it. At least not unless we keep it where it can't show on the mainland, in case your friends come back."

In late afternoon, Ben decided to go swimming off the little cove. Sandy went off to change into swim trunks, but Megan wasn't in the mood; she was too apprehensive, and she wanted to know the minute Grandpa returned from town. There wasn't any question now about telling him about the letter to Annie, the one *from* her, and the men who had come while he was gone. Grandpa would know what to do.

Whenever she thought of her letter to Annie, new guilt washed over her. Was it because of that letter, mailed in secret, that someone had been able to find them? They'd moved other times, when Mom hadn't left a forwarding address, hadn't told anyone where they were, and nobody had found them.

Tears stung her eyes. She wished her mother would come back, even if it meant they had to run again. She had always taken being part of a family—even a single-parent family—for granted. She didn't like having that family split up, even temporarily.

"Sure you don't want to come?" Ben asked, drawing her out of her reverie.

Ben still had both parents, and an extra father, but he didn't feel part of a family. She felt an unexpected twinge of sympathy for Ben.

"No. I'd better watch for Grandpa."

"OK." For once he.didn't try to bully her into complying with him. "When you see him, or my dad, come get us. We'll head for shore."

"Do you think your dad would help us?"

"Sure! He's really a good guy. It's only that the divorce wasn't his idea, and he's hurting from that, I guess. And he always gets uptight when he's writing to a deadline and it's not going as fast as he wants it to. Ready, Sandy? OK, let's go."

It was very quiet after the boys' voices died away. Megan sat on her airy perch as if she were a bird, high in the trees, able to see across the lake in all directions. It was a wonderful spot, and for a while she could pretend that it was all hers, that no one threatened its serenity.

When at last a car eased into sight in the yard beside the cottage, Megan grabbed for the binoculars. Grandpa's face jumped closer, and a feeling of relief swept over her. He had been shopping; he started unloading the car. He set down a bag and poked in the can of rocks, dumping some of them onto the boards of the porch; Megan remembered she'd put the key in her jeans pocket, and felt a moment's panic that it might have fallen out in the lake during one of her dunkings.

Grandpa gave up and got out another key, letting himself inside. Megan carefully hung the expensive binoculars on a projecting nail inside the tree house, then climbed rapidly down the ladder. "He's here!" she called, even before she was close enough for the boys to hear her. "Grandpa's home!"

# thirteen

"I WAS WONDERING where you kids had got off to," Grandpa said, busy putting away the groceries he had carried in. "I hoped maybe you'd have supper ready, since I was so late. Just in case, though, I brought fried chicken with me. I know your mom doesn't approve of fried foods, but once in a while . . ."

He turned then and saw Ben. "Oh, we got company?"

"Ben's dad's been gone all day," Megan said. Her mouth was dry with dread at the coming ordeal of confessing how foolish she had been about writing to Annie. "He hasn't come back yet. Is it OK if Ben stays?"

"Sure. Why not?" Grandpa said, but he wasn't smiling. A moment later they knew why. He nodded toward the table, and Megan saw two letters lying there. "I picked up the mail on the way in. Surprised me, you hadn't been out to get it. There's a letter there from your friend Annie."

Megan's throat felt as if it were closing, as if she were suffocating. Now she was in for it, and seeing how troubled her grandfather looked, she was ashamed that she hadn't trusted him in the first place and asked his advice about writing.

Ben and Sandy stood just inside the kitchen doorway, not speaking. It was up to Megan.

She reached for the letter, then recognized the handwriting on the other envelope. Her jaw dropped. "It's from Mom!"

"Yes." Grandpa's voice was level, serious. "How did Annie know where you are, Megan?"

Her legs were suddenly wobbly. Megan sank onto a chair. "I wrote to her," she admitted in a small voice. "I was going to tell you—I didn't realize it might mean somebody would ask about us at home, and *follow* us here. . . ." She sounded as if she might cry, but a quick glance at Ben made her determined not to do that.

"Follow you?" Was there alarm in Grandpa's voice?

It all came out then. The letter to Annie, Annie's response, and then the man in the white car, and the other two men in the blue Ford.

Grandpa listened so quietly, with so few interrupting questions, that Megan felt worse than ever, worse than if he'd shouted at her.

"You're sure none of them got into the house?" he asked when she finally fell silent.

"No, they didn't. Grandpa, I'm afraid they'll come back."

"Yes," he confirmed. "They probably will. I guess you weren't close enough to either of the cars to see the license plates?"

"The white car had Illinois plates—NC3–4289. The other one we thought had Minnesota plates. We only saw it through the binoculars, from the island, and we couldn't read the numbers."

"Illinois?" He said it sharply, as if that meant something to him, though he didn't explain. "Well, I wish you'd talked to me about writing to your friend, Megan. Your mother should have made it clearer, I guess, that you shouldn't contact anyone back home."

Megan's fingers crept across the table to touch the second letter. "There's no return address, but it's Mom's writing."

"Yes. I haven't had time to read it yet. Maybe we'd better see what these letters say. Open them up."

Megan read her mother's note first. She had already noted that the postmark was Ironwood, Michigan, which meant nothing to her except that her mother had apparently driven east.

Her lips felt stiff as she read aloud.

*Dear Dad and Kids:*

*I'm sorry to have left you so abruptly, and with no explanations. I'm feeling better about everything now; I just wanted you to be together while I looked for another job. Worrying about money doesn't do anything for my disposition, I guess. I think I've lined up a job; I'll know for sure in a couple of days. If it comes through, I'll be back to Lakewood to explain. Yes, Dad, I can see you're right. Megan and Sandy are old enough to understand, I hope. Anyway, I want them to have a fun vacation at the lake for a couple of weeks, and by then I'll have a house or an apartment here to bring them to. In the meantime, kids, have fun.*

*Love, Me.*

There was a postscript at the bottom of the page. *It might be better not to mention to anyone around there where this was postmarked, though it's not in the town where I'll be working.*

There was silence when she put the letter down on the table. Nobody asked why they weren't to mention the postmark. In a town the size of Lakewood, it was possible that the postmaster or the mail carrier had already noticed where the letter came from. Which also made it possible that one of those people would mention it to anyone who was asking questions about the Colliers.

Ben cleared his throat. Sandy shuffled his feet uneasily. Grandpa cleared his throat, too. "Maybe you better see what your friend Annie has to say."

Reluctantly, Megan tore open that envelope. She read the brief message to herself first, then out loud for the benefit of the others. The tears were there in her voice; she couldn't help them.

*"Dear Megan,"* she read. *"Mom said I'd better write to you again, in case any of this is important. Mrs. Morgan talked to Mrs. Salzman. . . .* She broke off to explain to Ben. "Mrs. Morgan was our next-door neighbor, and Mrs. Salzman lived next door to her." She swallowed and continued.

*"Mrs. Salzman said the night you left she saw a picture on TV, of two kids. The announcer said, 'Have you seen these children?' and there was a telephone number to call. Mrs. Salzman said they were just little kids, but she thought they looked remarkably like you and Sandy, though their name wasn't Collier. Anyway, my mom told her it was probably just coincidence, but that man*

· 114 ·

*was back in the neighborhood again today, and we saw Mrs. Morgan talking to him. We don't know what she said to him, but my dad was coming up the walk past them and heard the guy thank her for her help.*

*Megan, are you in trouble? I hope you can write and tell me everything's OK. I'll understand—well, sort of—if you can't write back again.*

*Love, Annie."*

Megan's worst fears were realized. She couldn't bear to look directly at her grandfather when she said, "I did it, didn't I? The man wouldn't have known where to look for us, if I hadn't sent the letter to Annie."

His reply was gentle. "Yes. But if your mother had told you why all this secrecy was necessary, you'd have known better, so don't take all the blame. I'm puzzled by the second car, the one with two men. I don't know who they could be."

Sandy spoke up, sounding croaky. "Was it our picture on TV? An old picture?"

"I didn't see it," Grandpa reminded. "It's possible."

"But those pictures asking 'Have you seen these children' are of kids who've been kidnapped, aren't they?"

For a moment Megan thought Grandpa wasn't going to answer that. Then he sighed. "Yes. This situation is leaving me in an intolerable position. Your mother wants to tell you what's going on herself. But if this man from Illinois is here looking for you—and maybe someone else is looking, too—then I'm not sure I can safely wait until she shows up to do it."

Safely. That was the key word. "Are we *not* safe?" Megan asked unsteadily.

Again Grandpa hesitated. "I don't know. I don't know if safe is the right word. I'm sure he doesn't intend to *harm* you. . . ."

"Who?" Megan demanded. "Who is the man from Illinois? You know who he is, don't you?"

"Not his name, no. I've no doubt who he's working for, though."

"Who?" Sandy blurted, while Ben watched with eyes that swung from one face to the other, alive with interest.

Grandpa eased into the chair opposite Megan, waving a hand at the boys. "Let's sit down. My foot's aching from being on it too much today, and I'm tired. If you're hungry, you might as well dig into that chicken and stuff."

Nobody made a move toward the cartons in the middle of the table, though Ben and Sandy did take chairs. Certainly food was the last thing on Megan's mind.

"What's the man going to do if he finds us?" Megan asked, her voice ragged with emotion. "Who is he working for?"

Grandpa sat for a moment, thinking out what he was going to say. He looked tired, so tired that once more guilt washed over Megan.

"Did you ever wonder," Grandpa asked at last, "about the *other* side of the family? Besides me and your mother?"

"You mean . . . Daddy's family? I thought they were all dead."

Grandpa shook his head. "No. You have one relative left on your dad's side of the family. A grandfather. He lives in Chicago."

It made Megan feel very strange. Another grandfather? Well, naturally she'd always known there had *been* another set of grandparents, but she'd assumed they had died before she was born. Her mother had never mentioned them.

In fact, Megan remembered distinctly that her mother had once stated that Grandpa Davis was their only living relative, aside from herself.

Sandy was looking confused. "A grandfather? But how come we never knew about him?"

"*That* I think you'll have to let your mom explain. She had her reasons for the things she did, and she hopes if she tells you herself you'll understand better. Megan, there's potato salad in that big carton, and cole slaw in the smaller one. Why don't you get us some napkins and paper plates, and we'll eat while we figure out what we ought to do."

Ben spoke for the first time, helping himself to a chicken thigh from the cardboard container. "Get out and go somewhere else," he said with his customary assurance of being right.

Grandpa shook his head. "If we leave here, there's no way for Karo to find us, and we don't know how to contact her. Besides, what's a crippled-up old man . . ." he thumped his cast on the floor, ". . . with no cash to speak of, going to do with two kids on the run? I have credit cards, but they're easy for a detective to trace."

"A detective?" Ben asked, pausing in his chewing. "Is that guy from Illinois a detective?" He seemed pleased with the idea.

"That's my guess. Hired by Daniel . . ." Grandpa broke off abruptly.

"Is that our grandfather's name? Daniel Collier?" Megan asked. She was extremely uncomfortable, as if she couldn't breathe properly.

"If I'm not careful I'm going to usurp your mother's right to explain things herself, the way she wants. Anyhow, I don't think running away again is a viable option. Besides the lack of cash, two redheaded kids and an old man in a cast are going to be noticed wherever they go. We wouldn't be hard to trace for a professional, only for my daughter."

"What'll he do if he finds us?" Sandy persisted. That question remained to be answered.

"I don't know. I only know that your mother doesn't want him to find you, doesn't want your grandfather to know where you are. It's her decision to make, not mine."

"Is that why we've been running away for eight years, ever since Daddy died?" Megan asked. She was still totally bewildered. Why should they have to hide from a grandfather they didn't know?

Grandpa took so long to reply that she almost gave up hope he was going to do it. "This is all very complicated, child. I don't know how to explain part of it without explaining it all, and I can't do that, not yet. When your mother comes, you can ask her anything you like."

"You just going to sit here and wait for the man to come back, then?" Ben wanted to know. He had helped himself to salads and more chicken, and was buttering a biscuit, the only one eating with any real appetite.

"If I knew any place to send the kids, I'd do it," Grandpa said, almost as if to himself.

"The island," Megan murmured. "We were on the island all day. There's no reason anyone would look for us on the island."

Grandpa's eyes were very blue under his thick gray eyebrows. "It might be for four or five days. . . ."

"We built a house," Sandy offered eagerly. "It's big enough for three sleeping bags, and we've got food out there. Well, it's Ben's food, but we could take some of our own. Nobody'd know where we were. You could come out there too, Grandpa!"

"No. I have to stay here. I can deal with this detective, or whoever he is. But if you think you want to try it, there's no danger out there that I can see."

"You could rig up some signals," Ben said. "Fly a red flag from the tree where you hang the life preservers if you wanted them to stay away. Fly a blue one if you wanted them to come in."

"If you fly flags somebody will figure out they're for signals," Megan pointed out.

"Hang up laundry in those colors," Ben said promptly. "A red shirt for a warning, a blue one meaning come ashore. String a clothesline between two trees right on the water, so we can see it from the tree house."

Grandpa thought it over. "All right," he said. "Maybe that would be a good idea. Just for tomorrow, to begin with. If the man comes back, I'll have a better idea of what to do after that, depending on what he says."

They ate then, though neither Megan nor her grandfather displayed a normal appetite. Grandpa found a box and began to put bread and peanut butter and strawberry jam and fruit into it. "You kids better pack up what you'll need to stay until at least tomorrow afternoon," he said over his shoulder. "How about you, Ben? You going to go home, or stay on the island, too?"

"I'll run home and leave a note for Dad, telling him I'm sleeping in the tree house," Ben said, without having to think it over.

It must be nice, Megan thought, to be able to decide so quickly and be sure you're right. *She* was confused, and just as apprehensive as she'd been before, because Grandpa Davis was obviously taking this matter very seriously. Somehow she had assumed that once she'd confessed to him, he would have everything under control.

"I'm going to take something to read," Sandy said, "and my pajamas."

"Take a clean set of underwear, too," Megan suggested. "And a clean shirt. You spilled catsup on that one."

She turned on the light in the small bedroom. It wasn't dark yet beyond the window that faced the lake, and she could see the island. She stood for a moment, studying it, trying to make out any telltale sign of the tree house, but it was too well hidden in the branches.

She sighed and picked up the tote bag Mom had used to carry various odds and ends. She couldn't imagine being relaxed enough to enjoy reading, but it might be a very long day if they couldn't come back to shore. She dropped the book she had been reading last night into the bag.

The packet with the writing materials was lying on the edge of the dresser, and as Megan opened the top drawer to find a clean set of clothes, she brushed against the packet. It slid to the floor, its contents scattering on the linoleum.

She muttered under her breath, packing clean jeans in case she got this pair wet again, a knitted shirt, and underwear. Maybe she'd better take a sweatshirt, too, she thought, in case it got cooler.

Finally, the small bag packed, she knelt to pick up the stuff that had spilled. Should she take some stationery so she could write to Annie? She had to thank her for the warning, even if it did come too late, even if she had to wait to mail her letter from some other place. This time she'd get permission to do it from Mom or Grandpa.

Some of the papers in the folder had slid under the edge of the bed. Megan, on hands and knees, scraped together everything she saw and began to put it all back together. Car registration papers, insurance papers, an official looking document. . . .

Megan paused, sitting back on her heels. She'd never seen this before; it made her curious enough to look more closely, because it seemed to have been caught in something and damaged, so that only part of the original remained.

Certificate of Birth, she read. The name was Margaret Anne Kauffman. Nobody she knew, she thought, and was already putting it into the folder when her eye caught the date—May sixteenth—and the year. . . .

Something constricted in Megan's chest. The birthdate was her own.

What did it mean? Why was her mother saving a birth certificate for someone named Margaret Kauffman, who had been born the same day and year as Megan?

She made a hasty search through the materials in the folder, looking for anything to shed more light on the matter, but there was nothing. Not her own birth certificate, nor Sandy's.

Megan's own middle name was Ann. She sat staring at the paper, then held it closer to read the rest of the information it contained, and felt a chill born of uncertainty and fear creeping over her.

Megan Ann and Margaret Anne. The same initials, though the last name was different. Collier and Kauffman.

Born of Caroline and Daniel Kauffman, read the smaller print.

Daniel . . . Grandpa Davis had said Daniel was their other grandfather's first name; he'd stopped before speaking the last name.

On the rare occasions when she'd spoken of him at all, her mom had called Daddy "Dan." But his last name hadn't been Kauffman, had it? Wasn't it Collier?

Megan whispered the names aloud, then sat in a frozen lump until Sandy shouted, "Come on, Megan, let's go!

We can leave as soon as Ben gets back! We want to get settled on the island before it gets dark!"

"I'm coming," she said, then folded the mysterious birth certificate and put it into the bag with the book and her clothes to study later, wondering if the wild suspicions that coursed through her mind could possibly be true.

# *fourteen*

MEGAN FELT numb, empty inside. She had never wanted to move away from one town where she had made friends to another place where she had to start all over again. But she had trusted her mother, had accepted the idea that the moves were necessary. Though theirs was a single-parent family, it *was* a family. And she had felt secure and safe within it.

Now she didn't feel safe or secure at all. She'd heard of kids who were abandoned by a parent, and she didn't think Mom would ever do that. She still believed her mother was really concerned about her and Sandy. But something was wrong, and there was no doubt that Karen Collier had been less than honest with her kids about any number of things.

How could that be, when Mom had always preached

honesty? Oh, Mom had explained that one hundred percent honesty wasn't always the best policy. It was permissible to tell someone her new hat looked great on her, even when you thought it was horrible. You didn't have to be truthful when you ate a neighbor's gift of a pie with a crust that couldn't be cut with a knife, let alone a fork. You didn't have to tell people they looked awful, even if they did, because that only made them *feel* awful, too. It might be a kindness to say you had another engagement when you just didn't want to do something with someone but hated to tell him that.

Megan knew about little white lies. Everybody told them, Mom had admitted, at one time or another. It could be OK when it was intended to protect someone else's feelings, though not when it was to protect yourself from the consequences of a guilty action.

Which category did Mom's lies fall into, Megan wondered as she loaded her small bag into the boat. If what she suspected was true, there was more involved here than *little* lies.

Wolf was jumping around, barking, ready for another ride. It didn't matter to him that jumping around in a boat had already dumped him into the water twice. In his eagerness to go, he nearly knocked Sandy down, and made him drop a thermos jug into the lake.

"Sit! Darn it, Wolf, *stay!*" Sandy howled. And the dog did sink onto his haunches.

Ben had returned, carrying a big flashlight and a flight bag that bulged with mysterious contents. He scowled. "We're not going to take him, are we? What if he starts barking like an idiot while we're out there, and the guy who's looking for you is here? He'll get a boat and check the islands."

Grandpa had come out with the box of supplies, which he handed over to Sandy. "He may have a point. Maybe the dog had better stay here with me. He might bark and give me a little warning if anybody comes snooping around again."

Sandy looked disappointed. "His name's Wolf," he reminded Grandpa. "He won't like it if we leave him here."

"I'll take him inside and give him something to eat," Grandpa offered. "Now you kids be careful. I'll string a clothesline as soon as you're out of sight, and hang a few things on it. I've got a bright red towel. If that's hanging up, don't come in to shore. Chances are if that fellow is seriously looking for you, he'll be back tomorrow. Then we'll know where we stand."

Ben, who seemed to be enjoying all this intrigue, said, "Come on, are we ready? Let's shove off."

Grandpa reached down to take Wolf's collar. "Come on, fella, let's go inside."

Wolf, however, knew perfectly well that he was being left behind. He barked more loudly than ever, trying to pull away.

Sandy's face was glum. "He doesn't understand why he can't come." He pushed off, then settled himself in the stern as Ben took up the oars.

Megan was in the bow, facing shore as they headed out across the water. Her mind was in a turmoil. The small bag she had packed was resting against her feet, and in it, she could not forget, was a birth certificate for someone named Margaret Anne Kauffman, who had the same birthday as her own. It couldn't just be coincidence, could it?

Her first thought was that it was her own birth certificate, that she'd been named Margaret Anne, and then her parents had adopted her and renamed her Megan. It made her feel strange, half sick and frightened. Lots of kids were adopted, of course, but their parents told them so, right from the beginning. Why shouldn't they? It was OK to know that your parents had *chosen* you to be their child.

Once, when they'd lived briefly in Milwaukee, Megan had gone to school with a girl named Shirley who had learned, at the age of ten, that she was adopted. She'd been very upset when she overheard two aunts discussing the matter. It had taken her some time to settle down, even after her parents told her they'd intended to tell her when she was grown up. Why, Shirley had asked, did they have to wait until then? Was there something shameful about being adopted?

Megan hadn't known Shirley very well, but she'd been sympathetic and curious, as well. She'd talked to her mother about it. Megan still remembered that Saturday afternoon when she and Mom had discussed adoption while they shared milk and warm oatmeal-raisin cookies in their sunny kitchen.

It wouldn't bother her to know she'd been adopted, Megan had thought, not if her mother was honest with her. After all, it meant her parents had wanted her, even if she hadn't been born to them in the first place.

Grandpa had dragged the protesting Wolf into the cottage. Megan watched them go without conscious thought, her mind on more important things.

No, it wasn't a question of adoption, she decided. She and Sandy looked so much alike that even strangers knew they were brother and sister. And her father had had red hair. There were no pictures of him. She'd often wished for one, and she'd asked about that once. Mom had said they'd been lost during one of their moves, she guessed.

Now Megan wondered if that was a lie, too, though she couldn't think why it should have been. But there were pictures of her, and of Sandy, and some of Mom, too, including snapshots taken with Grandpa and Grandma Davis when Mom was real little. Why would only the ones of Daddy have been lost?

And what about the names? Her own initials were the same as those of the girl on the birth certificate. She had been "born to Caroline and Daniel Kauffman."

Ben was saying something, but she paid no attention. Mom's name was Karen, and Daddy's name had been Dan. Dan was short for Daniel, and that was the name of the mysterious, unknown grandfather in Chicago. And Grandpa Davis never called Mom Karen, he called her Karo. Which sounded the same as the first part of Caroline. And while Collier started with a *C*, and Kauffman started with a *K*, both sounded the same when spoken aloud.

Megan knew she was jumping to conclusions, but they seemed so logical she was convinced her suspicions were true.

The birth certificate was her own. Only her name wasn't really Collier, but Kauffman. It made her feel stranger than ever, sort of sick to her stomach.

Everything she had taken for granted, all her life, was turned upside down. If she wasn't really Megan Collier, but someone named Margaret Anne Kauffman, it was scary. If Mom had told as big a lie as that, what else that Megan had believed in was false?

Why hadn't she asked Grandpa, before they left, if her grandfather's name was Daniel Kauffman? If he had refused to answer, she thought she might have read the truth in his face.

Whatever it was, Grandpa knew, she thought. Though

Grandpa might not have told the lies, he had kept silent about the truth. Did that mean Mom had very good reasons for what she had done? Or only that both the adults in Megan's life had deceived her for reasons of their own?

She thought about the new grandfather. Why should Mom be hiding her and Sandy from him? Was he an evil man in some way? He must be quite terrible if Mom felt she had to run and hide, then run again, for eight years. If he had hired a detective to search for them, what did he mean to do when he found them?

There were no answers, of course. Only more speculations.

"Hey! Megan, we're here," Ben said.

Megan came to with a start. They had arrived at the island.

"You carry that stuff," Ben said, "and Sandy can get that box. I'll manage the rest." He was giving orders, as usual. For once Megan didn't care. She wasn't thinking about Ben at all, only about herself and Sandy, and wondering what was going to happen next.

Twilight fell slowly across the island. Sandy and Ben set out the checkerboard after Megan declined to play a game of Clue. She knew she'd never be able to concentrate on any game. Instead she decided to go for a walk by herself, so she could think.

"Remember you don't want to be seen from the mainland, in case that guy comes back tonight instead of tomorrow," Ben warned.

Megan didn't bother to answer. She was already walking away. She sort of wished the island were bigger, now, though before she'd liked it the size it was. It was a relief just to get away from the boys, to be able to stop worrying about how she looked, or if she cried, or what Ben thought about her being scared.

"You're safe out here," he had pointed out to her only a few minutes ago.

There was a lot Ben didn't know, and she couldn't pretend to be interested in some stupid game while she was thinking about all of it.

For a long time Megan sat on the little beach in the cove, listening to the call of a loon, seeing an occasional fish jump. Thinking didn't seem to help anything, and after a while she simply let herself drift, not trying to figure it out, not trying to think of a solution. Solving the problem was out of the question anyway, until she knew what the source of the problem was. Mostly what she hoped was that her mother had a good explanation for what she had said and done, one that would prove she was the kind of person Megan had always felt her to be.

It was nearly dark when she finally made her way back to the tree house. The boys were just putting away the checkerboard.

"Have a cookie," Ben said, and even that sounded like an order.

Megan *was* hungry. She hadn't eaten much of Grandpa's chicken and salads. She took a cookie from the package Sandy offered.

"It got too dark to see," Ben told her through a mouthful of chocolate chip crumbs. "I didn't think we should light the lantern. Even if it sits on the floor, they might be able to see the glow of it on shore. We're going to go to bed and tell ghost stories, OK? And just in case of an emergency, we're going to sleep in our clothes."

"In case we have to move fast," Sandy supplemented, putting the game box on one of the shelves.

Megan didn't participate in the ghost-story telling. In fact, she didn't really listen to them. She hoped that Grandpa Davis was right in thinking he could handle that man if he came back.

Sandy and Ben were still giggling when she fell asleep. She woke later, feeling chilly, and zipped up her sleeping bag, then slept until the sun was well up in the sky.

While Megan fixed sandwiches for breakfast—they'd already decided not to risk being detected by building a fire that would send up a column of smoke—Ben looked over to the shore with his binoculars.

Just as Megan handed him a sandwich and juice in a cardboard carton, Ben yelped.

"He's back," he said. "The guy in the white car, with the Illinois plates—he's back!"

# *fifteen*

BREAKFAST was forgotten.

Megan knelt between the boys, conscious of the fact that only a thin fringe of boughs and leaves hid the trio from anyone who might have been looking their way.

Even without the binoculars, Megan was sure the car was the same one, the one that belonged to the man from Illinois. A detective, Grandpa Davis thought, who had searched them out on behalf of a grandfather they had not known existed until yesterday.

"Grandpa's coming out to meet him," Sandy reported unnecessarily.

"He's inviting the guy inside. He must not seem dangerous." Did Ben sound disappointed?

Megan had lost none of her own apprehension. The three

of them sat waiting, tense and expectant, for what seemed a long time and probably was no more than ten minutes.

Then Grandpa and the man came back into the yard. They exchanged a few words, the man got into the car, they talked a bit longer, and the man drove away.

Not exciting at all, Megan thought. She wished she could have overheard what they said to each other.

Grandpa stood alone in the yard until the car had gone. He looked out across the lake toward them, but gave no sign of seeing them. Then he walked back into the cottage and let Wolf out into the yard, where the dog ran wildly around, smelling the ground and the canoe, looking for them. Discouraged, Wolf finally lay down near the red canoe, big head drooping onto his paws as he stared mournfully out over the lake.

"He's gone," Sandy said, relieved.

Megan shook her head.

"Grandpa didn't hang out the blue shirt to signal for us to come ashore," she said.

The day passed slowly. They kept only an occasional eye on the cottage. Holding binoculars was hard work if they did it for more than a short time, and nothing moved along the lake shore.

They ate, then Megan tried to read but couldn't concentrate. Finally she took out the birth certificate and studied it, more convinced than ever that it was her own, that she was not Megan Collier at all but some stranger named Margaret Anne Kauffman.

"What's that?" Ben demanded when he finally noticed.

She hadn't wanted to talk about her latest discovery; to put her suspicions into words would make them all more real, and she didn't want them to be real. She wanted to be the person she'd always been, didn't want a mysterious grandfather who hired detectives, didn't want to be a girl whose picture was flashed on television screens with the words *HAVE YOU SEEN THIS CHILD?*

Yet maybe Ben and Sandy could explain her discovery away, she thought. Maybe if she told them, they would think of some other explanation.

They didn't. Ben read through the birth certificate, nodding. "Same date, same initials, names like your parents' names. It's from a hospital in Rhinelander, Wisconsin. Is that where you were born?"

Megan was getting a headache. "I was born in Wisconsin, I think. I don't remember that anyone ever told me which town."

"It all fits," Ben said. "Boy, this is crazy! You must have some idea of what it all means."

"I don't. Only that Mom kept moving us around, and now it looks as if it might be because this other grandfather has been trying to find us."

"Maybe he's a millionaire, and we're his heirs," Sandy suggested.

"Why would Mom run away from him for that reason?" Megan asked reasonably. "There has to be more to it than that."

"Was my birth certificate in the package, too?" Sandy wanted to know.

"I didn't see it. I suppose it might have been; I didn't go over everything. Or else Mom kept papers like that in something else, and grabbed mine and put it in with other stuff by mistake, because she was in a hurry. I'm pretty sure she didn't intend for me to see it."

They talked about it for a while, and nothing either of

the boys said made Megan feel any better. Finally, she had to change the subject before it all made her really sick.

"Where were you born?" she asked Ben.

"Duluth," Ben said promptly. "It's the only place I ever lived, until now."

Megan sighed. "We've lived in so many places. Gone to so many schools." No, that was getting back on the wrong subject. "What's it like, going to just one school, in the same place, all your life?"

"Well, as a matter of fact . . ." Ben hesitated, reaching down to scratch a scabbed-over mosquito bite on his bare ankle. ". . . I've been to three schools. I got kicked out of all of them, so I had to go to different ones. It was one of the things that made Lawrence mad, because he had to drive me to the last one."

Sandy regarded him in awe. "Are you kicked out now?"

Ben shrugged. "I guess so. Maybe Dad will let me live with him and go to school wherever he is, but I don't think he's decided yet where he's going to be this winter. He's rented the cottage through September, because here at the lake is a good quiet place for him to work. I doubt if he'll spend the winter here, though. I think the road gets closed because of snow, and he wouldn't want to walk in from the county road with supplies and everything."

"What did you do to get kicked out?" Sandy demanded.

Ben gave him a defiant look. "Last time, I was caught smoking in the boys' bathroom."

Megan couldn't help herself. "That sounds stupid."

Ben grinned. "Smoking, or being caught?"

"Both. Everybody knows smoking is stupid. It gives you cancer and heart trouble and all kinds of nasty things."

Then curiosity got the better of her. "Did you like smoking?"

He had scratched off the scab and now a trickle of blood ran down his ankle. He ignored it. "Nah, not really. I guess you're right, smoking's stupid. It tasted terrible, and I nearly strangled when I inhaled."

"Why did you do it, then?" Sandy asked, puzzled.

"Because it was against the rules."

"That sounds like a dumb reason," Megan commented.

"Yeah, well, when you break the rules," Ben told her seriously, "they call your folks. You know. Make them come in to school and talk about you. I thought maybe if they had to come in, somebody would realize . . . you know."

"No," Megan said. "I don't know. What? I wouldn't want my mom to be called in to talk about me."

His smile was brittle; Megan had the feeling that it could shatter, like fragile glass. The way, she thought suddenly, Mom's favorite salad bowl had shattered when she dropped it. Megan knew, now, what had probably caused her to do it; she'd been frightened by seeing a picture of Megan and Sandy on TV, and the caption *HAVE YOU SEEN THESE CHILDREN?* That was why they'd left in such a hurry, because Mom was afraid the neighbors would see the picture and recognize it, too.

Ben was answering her statement. "That's because your mom already talks to you, right? She doesn't act as if you aren't there except when she says, 'For heaven's sake, use your fork,' or 'Ben, it's time to go to bed.' Your mom doesn't have a boyfriend, or a new husband, that resents every bit of attention she pays to you. Your mom doesn't shut you out, as if you weren't even part of the family."

Megan just looked at him, and Ben had the grace to blush.

"Well, usually, I mean. What's going on now is different. She's kept secrets from you, but it was to protect you, not because she doesn't care about you."

"I'm sure your mother cares about you, Ben. She got worried when you were late getting home from the beach, didn't she, or they wouldn't have called the police."

"She was mad when I saw her. More mad than worried. Lawrence was even madder. I think he'd have hit me if she'd let him."

"If she didn't let him," Sandy said helpfully, "it must mean she cares *some*."

Ben hadn't considered that, apparently. And he'd decided he didn't want to talk about himself anymore, the same as Megan had decided.

"Let's go swimming," Ben said. "We'll wait outside while you change first, Megan."

"What about Grandpa's signal? Maybe we can go ashore soon."

"And maybe it'll be hours before he puts up the signal for that. Maybe the guy is coming back. After all, he didn't get what he came for, did he? Come on, there's no sense in dying of boredom while we wait."

He had a point. Megan allowed herself to be persuaded, though she was anxious to return to the cottage and find out what had happened. She put on her swimsuit, then waited for the boys, and they all headed for the little cove.

The sand under their feet was soft and warm; the water was still pretty cold. Still, after they'd been in it for a few minutes, Megan decided she wasn't going to turn blue after all. For a short time she was able to enjoy the splashing and cavorting around.

As soon as they came out of the water, however, she was the first one back at the tree house, snatching up the binoculars as soon as she'd reached the platform.

There was the cabin, and there was the area where Grandpa had stretched the clothesline, and there . . .

She turned excitedly to the boys, who were climbing the ladder behind her.

"The signal is out! We can go home!" she cried.

They didn't even wait to get dressed, but scrambled to the ground and ran toward the boat.

GRANDPA AND WOLF were waiting for them on the beach. Wolf barked his welcome, swimming out to meet them. Sandy had to push him off to keep him from trying to climb into the boat, and when they disembarked the dog leaped around them, licking whatever part of any person he could reach.

"Who was he?" Sandy asked eagerly, turning toward Grandpa Davis. "Was he a detective?"

"Yes," Grandpa said. Megan noted uneasily that he didn't look either relieved or happy. "His name's Jules Picard, and he's from Chicago, just as I thought."

Megan was once more very tense. "And was he hired by . . . our other grandfather, to find us?"

"Yes. He didn't make any bones about that."

"What did you tell him?" Ben demanded.

"I told him it was true you'd been here, but that now you were gone. Without actually lying, I gave him the impression that your mom had come and taken you away, and I could truthfully state that I didn't know where she was. He assured me that he wished to cause no trouble—he says your grandfather doesn't wish that, either—and that he'd probably be in touch with me again after he'd reported to your grandfather. He wants me to persuade your mother to talk to him, at least. I think maybe that's what she ought to do, and put an end to this everlasting running and hiding. It's quite possible that Daniel actually has had a change of heart. After all, he's past seventy, and he can't expect to live forever. Maybe it's true that he really does want to mend his fences while there's still time."

"What's mend his fences mean?" Sandy asked uncertainly.

"Make amends for problems he's caused in the past. Make friends of his enemies. Make his peace with the world—and his grandchildren—before it's too late."

"Are we his enemies?" Sandy asked, looking worried.

"No, but he and your mother had a falling out, years ago, and . . . well, there I am again, trying to explain what your mom has said *she* wants to explain. The thing is, I'm not sure Mr. Picard believed me, about your mother having taken you away. He probably went into town to call Daniel and give him a report. I waited a few hours to see if he'd come right back, and he didn't, so I thought I'd better call you in. If we hear a car, though, get out of sight until I can decide what to do next. Until I'm sure what your mother will want to do, I'd rather they think you really aren't here."

Megan was trembling again. She ignored Wolf, who was affectionately licking her bare thigh. She couldn't wait until her mother came to know *anything*, and it wasn't fair that she should be expected to.

"Is our grandfather's name Daniel Kauffman?" she wanted to know.

For a moment she thought he wouldn't answer. "How did you learn that?" he asked at last.

And then she told him about the document she had found among her mother's papers. "It's *my* birth certificate, isn't it?"

For a long time there was silence. Even Wolf stopped jumping around and sat down, watching their serious faces.

"Oh, dear. Karo, love, if you want to do your own explaining," Grandpa said, as if Mom were there to hear him, "you'd better show up pretty soon. You've put me in an impossible position. This isn't fair to anybody."

"I'm . . . really Margaret Anne Kauffman," Megan persisted. The sick feeling was back, stronger than ever, and she felt as if she might throw up.

Grandpa's reply was indirect. "We called you Meg. That's sometimes a nickname for Margaret. And when your Mom decided it would be better to change it, she called you Megan, because it was as close as she could come to your real name."

Sandy moved closer, as if to draw comfort from Megan. She felt the warmth of his arm as it touched her own.

"Did she change my name, too?" he whispered.

Grandpa sighed, and then seemed to make up his mind. "All right," he said. "Let's sit down, let me get off this foot. I'll try to make you understand some of it, enough, I hope, to last you until your mom gets here. Here, on the porch will do."

At last, Megan thought. Finally someone was going to tell the truth.

She felt sicker than ever, though, and she wondered if

she really wanted to hear the truth. Maybe it would spoil everything for them all, would take away everything she'd thought their family had in the way of love and trust and affection.

She almost cried out—*No, don't!*—but the words were stuck in her throat, and she sank onto a step beside Grandpa's knee and waited for him to begin.

## sixteen

SANDY SAT two steps below Megan, looking up at his grandfather. "Grandpa? Am I somebody different, too?"

Grandpa seemed to be having trouble figuring out where to begin. He stretched out the foot with the cast on it, trying to get more comfortable. When he spoke, his voice was gruff.

"Your name was Andrew. When you were a toddler, we called you Andy. That got changed to Sandy, so it would sound different, yet not so different we couldn't remember to say *Sandy*."

From the look on his face, the news that his name had been changed didn't make Sandy feel any better than it had made Megan feel.

"And Mom's name is really Caroline," Megan said, when

Grandpa stopped speaking and couldn't seem to get started again. "Not Karen. That's why you call her Karo."

Grandpa grimaced. "It's hard to call your daughter by a name that's different from the one she grew up with. I always started with *Caro*. I wouldn't remember *Karen* until I'd already said it wrong to begin with, so I finally gave up and settled for something halfway between the two names."

Ben stood leaning against one of the posts that supported the porch roof. He spoke from over their heads. "There's somebody coming."

At the same moment Wolf leaped up, barking, sending Megan's heart into her throat. She was halfway to her feet, ready to flee into the house before the car came into the clearing, when Sandy—or should she think of her brother as Andy, Megan wondered in confusion—cried out.

"It's Mom!" he said, bounding down the lower steps. "It's Mom!"

The car was, indeed, familiar. It jounced over the bumpy spot in the driveway and rolled to a stop.

Mom looked the same as ever—well, better than when they'd last seen her. She was smiling, waving a hand out the window before she got the door open.

Grandpa pulled himself up, awkwardly because of the foot that couldn't bend inside the cast, and stumped after Sandy to meet his daughter. Ben stayed where he was, and so did Megan.

Her heart was pounding. A part of her was glad that Mom had come, that she was all right and that now *she* could answer the questions.

Mostly what she felt, though, she couldn't have described. Fear and anger and confusion. What possible reason could Mom have to change her name, make her another person from the one she should have been?

For a few moments Megan wasn't sure she liked her mother well enough to sit still and talk to her, or listen to her.

When her mother got out of the car, though, and kissed first Sandy and then Grandpa before she came toward the house, Megan reluctantly rose.

"Hi, honey. I'm back, I got the job, and I have a lead on an apartment, too. It won't be vacant until the fifteenth of July, but if you're having fun here with Grandpa that'll be soon enough to move anyway, won't it?"

She started to reach for Megan to give her a hug, then hesitated. "Is there something wrong?" she asked, sobering.

"You got here just at the right time," Grandpa told her. "We sort of reached a crisis point, where I was going to have to explain some things to the kids. I'm darned glad you came; you can have the job yourself."

And then, to Megan's astonishment, he clumped up the steps, past Ben, and into the house. Was Grandpa angry with Mom, too?

"Crisis?" Karen Collier echoed the word in alarm. "What's happened?"

"There's a detective looking for us," Sandy said. "From our other grandfather."

At the same time, Megan said, "I found my birth certificate."

Consternation swept over her mother's face, and she put out a hand to the rail beside the steps to steady herself, as if her legs might give way beneath her. "Oh, dear."

She stared into Megan's face, not far below her own. "Oh, honey, I'm sorry. I was going to tell you, I really was, only I couldn't bring myself to do it yet, not until I knew we had somewhere to go, some way to support our-selves. . . ."

She rested a hand on Megan's shoulder, then reached out for Sandy, too. "What's this about a detective? Tell me what's happened."

Megan found herself unable to speak. She wasn't sure whether it was relief that her mother had returned; resent-ment over the troubles her mother had left them with; or the devastating idea that she wasn't really Megan Collier, that there *was* no such person as Megan Collier.

Grandpa came out of the house carrying two steaming cups. "Thought maybe you'd need this," he said, handing over one of them. "Hold mine, son, while I get a couple of chairs," he said in an aside to Ben. It was not until both the adults were seated on chairs from the kitchen that anyone spoke again. Then Grandpa said, "All right, Karo. You'd better start from the beginning, and don't leave anything out this time."

She sipped cautiously at the coffee, visibly composing herself, but not being entirely successful. "All right. Only first can I know what the crisis is? What's this about a detective?"

"Name's Jules Picard," Grandpa said. "Hired by Daniel Kauffman. The man was here yesterday and today. Daniel wants to see his grandchildren."

For a few seconds Mrs. Collier closed her eyes. "No." The word was soft, in fact barely audible, yet it was firm. "No, Dad."

Grandpa ignored her response. "This Picard said that Daniel wants you to talk to him, at least. He says he is not threatening you, has no intention of causing any trouble for you or the kids. He only wants to talk to you, to try to persuade you to let him see the kids."

"Oh, it's 'persuade' now, is it? Not threaten? Not intimidate?" There was both pain and bitterness in her face and voice.

"Daniel is past seventy now, Karo," Grandpa said evenly. "A man can change, can consider different viewpoints, when he's getting on in years. His son is gone. Megan and Sandy are all he has left."

"They're all I have left, too, except you. I won't give them up, Dad."

"He's not asking you to. Not anymore. He only wants to see them."

Megan had never seen hostility flare in her mother this way, certainly not against Grandpa Davis. "So you're taking his side this time, are you?"

"No. I'm not taking any side at all. I'm simply trying to tell you what this Picard wanted you to know, what Daniel Kauffman wants you to know."

"I don't owe a thing to Daniel Kauffman," Mrs. Collier said, and her head came up in a defiant way.

"No, I don't think you do. But maybe you owe something to the kids. Maybe they've got a right to see their grandfather before it's too late."

Megan's stomach was churning, and she couldn't stop shaking; she felt weak and queasy. Her voice shook, too. "I want to know why you changed me from Margaret to Megan, to somebody that's just made up, not real at all!"

The hardness went out of her mother's face. "I'm sorry, Megan, I never planned anything the way it turned out. I only did what I felt I had to do at the time. It was all for your benefit, and Sandy's. I wanted to do what would be best for you."

There was pleading in the words. Megan wondered if she were supposed to melt at that. All she really felt was a fierce need to know the truth—and a fear of knowing, all at the same time.

Mom took another drink of the coffee, then set the cup on the porch rail. "OK," she said. "It's time you knew. You're old enough to make your own decisions on this, maybe. The thing you have to understand is that when it began, you *weren't* old enough. You were just babies, and I had to decide for you."

Megan waited, unwilling to admit there might be something valid in what her mother had said.

Her mother sighed, then drew a deep breath. "Your father's name was Daniel Kauffman, Jr. He was the only son of Daniel Kauffman, Sr., who was a very wealthy man who had great plans for his son. There had been a daughter, too, but she was killed in an accident when she was twelve. That made him even more determined that Danny—that's what we called your father—should have the best of everything. As his father saw it, anyway."

It was obvious that telling this was difficult. While Mrs. Collier spoke, her fingers twisted her skirt, pleating and unpleating it.

"Danny and I met, and fell in love. We wanted to get married, but his father didn't want him to marry me. When we did it anyway, your grandfather was furious. He told your father that he would be on his own, that there would be no more Kauffman money to make life comfortable.

"We said, 'OK, we don't need your money,' and we meant it. We were happy those first few years, or I thought we were. Poor, but we never went hungry. We were both thrilled when Megan was born. She was such a beautiful baby, with Danny's red hair. And a little over a year later, we had Sandy, who was beautiful, too. I thought that the life that stretched ahead of us looked wonderful, even if we did sometimes have difficulty keeping up with the bills."

She was speaking directly to Megan now, silently begging her to understand. "Then things seemed to get easier. Your father got a promotion at the office where he worked. At least he said he did. He brought home more money, and we bought a house, and a better car. We bought things for you kids, though you were too young to need much besides food and clothes, and we'd always given you those. And then I found out . . ."

Karo Collier swallowed, and it was impossible not to see that this was increasingly painful for her. "I found out that Danny hadn't been promoted, after all. He was . . . embezzling from his company, using the money to give us a better standard of living."

"Embezzling?" Sandy echoed, incredulous. "You mean stealing?"

"Yes. Stealing. I found out by accident, and I didn't want to believe it, but when I faced him with it . . ." She had to swallow again. "He acted as if it were no big deal. He'd been rich, spoiled, all his life. He didn't see why he should have to give up all those luxuries, why he should have to struggle."

Megan felt numb. Her daddy, the beloved daddy of her imagination, had been an embezzler, a thief? She felt as if her world had suddenly tilted sharply, so that she was about to slide off into an abyss. She dug her fingernails into her palms as if to hold on.

"I pleaded with him to talk to his father, to confess and ask for help in replacing the money he'd taken, before he was caught. He finally did, only Daniel Kauffman, Sr., didn't see it that way. In effect, what he told Danny was, 'You've made your bed, now lie in it.' A month later, Danny's employer discovered the shortage, and Danny lost his job. They couldn't prove he'd taken the money, so they didn't bring charges against him, but they fired him.

"It was frightening. We couldn't make our house payments, and Danny couldn't get another job. Not without a reference from his old employer, who wouldn't give it. So he . . . he held up a bank."

Megan felt as if her heart had stopped. Her chest ached, and her breathing almost stopped. Sandy was staring at his mother with horrified eyes.

"They caught him with the money still on him." Now Mrs. Collier sounded stolid, controlled. Megan glanced at Grandpa, and saw that he had known about this for a long time, that he felt compassion for what his daughter had gone through. "There was a trial, and he was convicted, and sentenced to prison. Your father had . . . had shot a teller. He only wounded her, so the charge wasn't . . . as bad as it would otherwise have been, but he'd used a gun to commit a felony. He would be in prison a long time. And I . . ." Suddenly her voice broke. It was several moments before she spoke again.

"We lived in a small town. Everybody knew about it, and I felt ashamed, disgraced. I had thought I loved Danny, but now I didn't know anymore. Could I love someone who would shoot an innocent woman in order to rob a bank? I didn't know. I packed up you kids and moved in with Grandpa and Grandma Davis, in a different town where nobody knew me. That's when I told the first lie." Her gaze met Megan's again. "I let people there think I was a widow. That my husband had died. I got a job to try to support you kids."

Was she trying to tell Megan that the first one had been a little white lie? To protect the children, even more than herself? A lie that hurt no one?

"Then Daniel Kauffman came to visit me. I hadn't seen him since Megan was born, though he knew about both of you. He said I wouldn't be able to take care of two kids, and he offered to take you and care for you. I told him no."

Megan wished an image of this grandfather would form in her mind. Had he been redheaded, like Daddy? Did he have a kind face, or a stern one? Was his voice gentle, or gruff? From what her mother had said, she didn't think he had been either kind or gentle.

"Two days later," her mother was continuing, "I lost my job. I never knew for sure, but I thought Daniel Kauffman was behind it. Probably all he'd have had to do was tell my boss that my husband was in prison for bank robbery and assault, even though I had nothing to do with that. Anyway, I had to hunt for another job.

"Maybe the word got around about my true background. At any rate, I couldn't find another position in that town. At first Daniel Kauffman just kept pestering me, to let him take you kids. Then he filed suit to take you away from me."

The words were ugly, chilling. What kind of grandfather was this, who would take young children away from their mother?

"I had no job. No money for lawyers. I had lost my husband. All I had left was you and Sandy, Megan. Can you understand how I felt? Your grandfather was rich enough to hire half the lawyers in Chicago if he wanted them. He said I couldn't take adequate care of you kids, and that he only wanted to see that you were well cared for. Until I got on my feet."

The bitterness was back, and she didn't try to conceal it. "The trouble was, with all the tension and anxiety, I got sick. I wasn't crazy, but I was foolish. I said some wild things in front of other people. Daniel Kauffman tried to have me committed to a mental hospital. The doctors finally said I didn't belong there, but not until after they'd held me for seventy-two hours' observation. I was so angry and distraught it's a miracle they *didn't* decide I was having a nervous breakdown."

She cast a glance at her father, as if seeking his confirmation. He nodded ever so slightly.

"Grandpa didn't have the money for lawyers, either, but he had a friend who managed to get me released, so he could take me home. I was afraid by that time that Daniel would do *anything* to take my children away from me. I became convinced that he *would* take you, with his expensive lawyers and his testimony that I was unstable, unfit to care for young children. So I panicked and ran. I packed up your clothes, and put the two of you in my old car, and I ran."

Megan stared at her mother, not knowing whether she felt sorrow for her or only bewilderment.

Her mother had run away, and kept on running, for eight years.

Her father hadn't died eight years ago. He had gone to jail for robbing a bank and shooting a teller.

Megan closed her eyes against the tears that came, and felt them trickle through, then run down her cheeks.

## *seventeen*

ALL HER WHOLE LIFE, Megan thought, she would remember this hour. She would remember the warmth of the boards of the porch steps, and the chirping of some small bird in a nearby birch, and the sound of Mom's voice, telling her these impossible things. The things that hurt so much by themselves, and were made worse by the fact that the mother she had always thought so perfect had lied to her.

She would remember the shine of tears in her mother's eyes as Karen Collier leaned toward her, as if she wanted to reach out and touch Megan but no longer felt she had a right to do so.

"Surely you can understand why I didn't try to explain anything to you at first," she begged. "You were too little to understand, only babies! And then the time never came when it seemed right to tell you. . . . It's very hard to say to a child, 'Your father is a criminal, he's in jail,' and what good would it have done? It would only have been hurtful."

Did she think it wasn't hurtful now? Megan wondered dully. What would the other kids think, if they knew? Would they say cruel things and avoid her, as if it were her fault? Would anyone, even Annie, still like her? At the moment, Megan didn't like herself. She didn't want to be Megan Collier, or Margaret Anne Kauffman, either.

Was that how her mother had felt? That she didn't want to be the wife of a man who had held up a bank and shot someone?

The thought pricked at her like a sharp sliver, and Megan pushed it aside.

"Is he still there?" she asked, sounding muffled. "Is Da— my father, is he still in prison?"

It hurt so terribly, to say the words. Even worse than hearing her mother admit that she had told lies. How could these things be true about the laughing redheaded man who had tossed her into the air and caught her, the man she was almost sure she really remembered, not just imagined?

Her mother wiped impatiently at the tears that spilled over, with the back of her hand, as if she were a child. "No," Mrs. Collier said quietly. "He died there, just a few months ago. Not violently, nothing like that. He just got sick and died."

So the dreams had ended, once and for all, and Megan could never think of her father again as a loving man who would have been like Annie's dad, if he'd lived.

"I thought it was all over, then," Mrs. Collier said, sighing. "That maybe, somehow, we could stop running. That

I could stop watching the papers for his name, being afraid that he'd been paroled, that he'd robbed another bank or something."

She glanced at her father. "I don't know how many times, over the years, I thought Daniel Kauffman was about to catch up with us. For over a year we didn't even see Grandpa and Grandma Davis, and I wrote to them at a post office box, under an assumed name, to make it harder for anyone to trace us. By the end of that year, they had moved to another town, too, and I thought it was safe for a while. Then I saw a man I thought was watching our house, and I spooked and ran again. Grandpa Davis thought I imagined some of the things that made me think Daniel Kauffman was still looking for us. Maybe I did, I don't know, but I couldn't take the chance. This whole last year nothing had happened, and then I read that tiny piece in the paper about your father's death, and I thought it was all over. I didn't have to worry anymore."

She sipped at her coffee, which must have cooled off by this time. "That lasted until I saw the picture on TV, the picture that still looked like you two, even though it was taken so long ago. And I realized Daniel Kauffman was looking for you again, or still. That Danny's death didn't mean it was all over, only that his father would never have his son back, so he wanted his grandchildren. Not that he ever gave up wanting you, I suppose, but now he was going to really try hard to find you. I took it for granted that if he were doing that, he'd use his money and his influence to try to take custody away from me, the same as he tried before."

Sandy cleared his throat. "Don't we have anything to say about what happens? Doesn't it matter who *we* want to be with?"

Mrs. Collier reached out and hugged him. "Of course it does! Only he can offer you so much, and I . . . I haven't done very well in what I've been able to give you, have I? I guess I've always been afraid that you'd *want* to go with him, to that big house and all that money. . . ."

Her voice broke, and for a few seconds she and Sandy clung together.

"We'd never want to leave you, Mom," he said, sounding gruff with emotion.

Mrs. Collier managed a teary smile, speaking over the top of his head. "Can you try to understand, Megan? I thought I was protecting you. And now Daniel's detective has caught up with us. Though he doesn't know we're here right this minute, does he? We could still follow through on my plan, go to a new town, take the new job, and hope he doesn't find us again. . . ."

"Karo," Grandpa Davis said gently. "All Daniel has said is that he wants to talk to you. According to this Mr. Picard, he doesn't want to take the kids away from you, he only wants to see them. Wants to make them part of his life. You can't blame him too much for that. You've proved that you can take care of the kids, that you're a good mother. Even his money can't argue against that. He probably couldn't get custody of Megan and Sandy now if he *did* take the matter to court, and he's sworn he won't do that."

"And you think I should talk to him." Mrs. Collier sounded subdued.

Grandpa hesitated. "Yes, since you've asked me, that's what I think. In the meantime, until you decide, we'll just pretend the kids aren't here, if Picard comes back. So where's the risk? Daniel isn't going to give up looking, if you disappear again, so you'd eventually have to go through all of this another time. And think how it would feel to stop running and hiding."

Ben, who had listened to all this without speaking, suddenly moved from where he was leaning against the post at the top of the steps. "Uh, I guess I better go on home and see if Dad found my note. I'll see you later, guys."

Megan leaped up, too. "I'll walk partway with you," she offered. She didn't want to sit there any longer and hear more things that would frighten her, make her heart ache. She didn't want to look at her mother's face.

Megan bounded down the steps, not looking back, and Ben trotted at her side. Neither of them said anything until they were on the beach, heading toward his house.

"I almost wish I didn't know the truth about my father," Megan blurted. "Who's going to like me, if they know?" She couldn't even think of him as *Daddy* anymore; he was a stranger, a horrid stranger who had done terrible things.

"Kids aren't going to dislike you because of your father," Ben said halfheartedly. And then, when she flashed him an angry glare, he shrugged and admitted, "Well, maybe some of them will. They're the stupid ones, though. The ones worth having as friends will like you for yourself."

"Kids can be cruel," Megan said. "They make fun of people who are different—someone who limps, or has to wear glasses, or can't talk plain. Or someone whose mother is fat, or whose father is in prison."

Ben jammed his hands into the pockets of his jeans, looking at the sand rather than at her. "Yeah," he agreed. "Some kids are real jerks. But they aren't the ones you'd want to be friends with anyway. I wouldn't stop being friends with somebody because their dad's a bank robber."

He considered that, before adding, "Maybe my mother would. I mean, she might not want me to associate with a bank robber's kids. But I'd do it anyhow."

"You're different," Megan said, and knew it was true, and that she didn't resent Ben any more. He'd already proved he was a friend.

Ben laughed, though not in a way that suggested he really thought it was funny. "You're right there. I've been kicked out of three schools because I'm different. My stepfather can't stand me, my mom thinks I'm a nuisance, and my dad's too busy to notice me except when I do something that makes him mad. Listen, just because you know about your dad now doesn't mean you have to have a bumper sticker made about it or wear a sign on your forehead. Just say he's dead, that's the truth, and let it go at that."

Megan supposed he was right. Ben was usually right, or thought he was. He knew how to solve everybody's problems—except, she suddenly realized, his own.

Megan made a small, strangled sound. Her mom *did* care about her, for all that she'd kept so many things secret, and so did Grandpa Davis . . . and maybe this new grandfather would, too, though he'd been so mean before that she didn't know if she believed that. "I guess I'll live," she said finally.

"Yeah. Me, too," Ben said. "Listen, we don't have to go back to the island to hide, so why don't we go swimming after a while? After you get through talking to your mom and everything."

"Sure," Megan said. She didn't really feel like doing anything, but sitting around thinking wasn't going to make things any better.

"Well, there you are, Ben. I wondered if I'd ever see you again."

They had walked right up on Mr. Jamison without Megan noticing. He was sitting on the beach, and the Irish setter lay panting beside him.

He was a very good looking man, Megan thought, for a moment remembering the image she'd had of her own father, of the kind of man she'd thought him to be. Mr. Jamison looked nice, too.

"This must be Megan," Ben's father said, getting to his feet and brushing sand off his slacks. "Is there something going on I don't know about?"

Ben looked at Megan. "Well, yeah. I guess. I'll tell you later. I'm going to have something to eat, and then after a while we're going swimming."

"Good. I've got a pot roast cooking for supper, be ready pretty quick now. You want to stay for supper, Megan?" Mr. Jamison invited, smiling.

Ben was astonished. "How come you're cooking? How come I can have company for supper?"

"Because I finished my book, and now I can be a human being until I start the next one. Oh, I still have to do the revision, but that's the easiest part. No doubt Megan has heard that I'm the Jamison dragon, breathing smoke and fire. Don't believe it, Megan. I only do that when I'm working hard to meet a deadline, and the younger dragon in the family is inconsiderate about the demands he makes on me. Like wanting meals on time, cooked meals. Anybody who's twelve should be able to shift for himself in that department, shouldn't he?"

Megan didn't know what to say. Mr. Jamison didn't *seem* disagreeable. "Thank you, but I have to go home. My mom's here, and I don't know how long she'll stay. We have sort of a . . . a crisis, I guess, right now."

Mr. Jamison nodded. "I know all about crises. If I don't

have one of my own, my son creates one for me. We thrive on crises, don't we, Ben?"

He rested one hand on Ben's shoulder. Ben's face had lighted up, which made him look quite different from the way he usually did.

"Does this mean I can talk to you tonight?"

"You can talk," his father agreed. "We'll see you again, Megan."

She walked home thoughtfully. She hoped Ben and his father worked it out, that maybe Ben could stay with him and go to school instead of having to return to Duluth and the stepfather who didn't like him and the mother who thought he was a nuisance. Knowing about Mr. Jamison only from Ben's viewpoint had made her not like the man very well, but he'd seemed OK just now. It made her suddenly wonder if her view of her mother was distorted, too. She felt peculiar and uneasy about that.

She plodded slowly home over the sandy beach. She didn't want to really talk to her mother again until her own emotions were sorted out.

When they were getting ready for bed that night, Megan stood stiffly as Mrs. Collier hugged her.

"You haven't forgiven me, have you?" her mom asked quietly.

"I don't know. I guess you did what you thought was right," Megan responded. "I'm just all mixed up. Everything I believed about Daddy—about my father—wasn't true. I'm not even the person I thought I was."

"Honey, your name doesn't make you a different person. You're still *you*."

"I don't feel like me," Megan said sadly.

This time when her mother's arms came around her,

however, she accepted the hug, though she didn't hug back.

Later, lying in the bed while her mother slept beside her, Megan watched the shadows move across the window as the moon rose over the lake. She heard the loons with their mournful cries, and something else.

Suddenly she was wide awake, heart racing.

A car coming in off the main road?

Swiftly Megan slid out of bed, making her way by moonlight through the house, sliding back the bolt so she could open the kitchen door onto the side porch.

Yes, there was a car, a car that sounded as if it needed a tune-up, because it rattled and spluttered as the ignition was turned off, not far away.

Not Mr. Jamison. His sleek black Porsche hummed like a contented cat. Mom's car, and Grandpa's, stood in the yard, so it wasn't one of theirs.

Who, then?

She jumped when Wolf pressed his wet nose into her hand. "Shh!" she told him, listening intently. Why would anyone come so near and not go on to either of the places on this road where anyone was living?

She heard nothing more. No voices. Though she stood for some time in the doorway, no one appeared in the clearing in the moonlight. After a while Megan closed and relocked the door and went back to bed. She heard Wolf's toenails clicking on the linoleum-covered floor as he returned to Sandy's room.

He hadn't barked. She thought he'd have barked if anyone had come close to the house.

It wasn't until she had crawled in beside her mother that the thought struck her.

Grandpa had talked to the detective from Illinois, but what about the two men in the blue car with Minnesota plates? They had come while no one was home, had snooped around trying doors and looking in windows, and driven away again. Where did they fit into the picture? Surely the man named Daniel Kauffman hadn't sent *two* sets of detectives to find them.

Who were they, then? Why had they come, and would they be back? Were they in that car that had stopped out there in the darkness and not yet driven away?

Megan did not fall asleep for what seemed a long time, and she never did hear the car leave.

In the morning she told everybody about the car.

Her mother looked rested, more relaxed, this morning. She put an arm around Megan and hugged her.

"I wouldn't worry about it, honey. Chances are you just heard someone parking in what they thought was a private place, to talk, maybe. Or a young couple, courting."

"But what about the two men? They acted just like the detective. They didn't know we were watching them from the island, and they tried the doors and looked in the windows."

"Looking for something to steal, maybe," Grandpa said. "I don't suppose they saw much worth breaking in for in this place. Here, who wants the first pancake?"

They weren't taking it seriously, Megan thought. Maybe they were right.

Yet her uneasiness remained.

# eighteen

DURING BREAKFAST Mom told them about the new job, which she thought she was really going to like. She told them about the town where they'd be going to live, too, though she didn't give them the name of it, only a description.

"It's on Lake Michigan. The apartment I looked at didn't work out, so I'm going to try to find a house that's within walking distance of the water, so you can go to the beach," she said as she began to clear the table.

Sandy sat up straighter. "A house? Mom, if we get a house instead of an apartment, can we keep Wolf? Can we take him with us?"

Megan thought of how the dog had crouched with her in the woods when she watched the detective, and how he had come to her side last night when she'd been frightened by the sounds of that car.

"He's a nice dog," she said, and earned Sandy's grateful look. "And he eats everything."

Her mother gave a rueful laugh. "That's what I'm afraid of. He's a big dog, and he'll eat a lot. Buying dog food might mean more tuna casseroles instead of more hamburgers."

Wolf seemed to know he was under discussion. He thumped his tail, watching closely as the plates were scraped into his dish.

"I don't know, Sandy. We'll have to wait and see. If we have a place in town, it would have to have a fenced yard. I don't believe in letting dogs run loose where they can get into traffic and maybe be hit."

Sandy hesitated, then decided to let it rest. He brought up another subject that Megan, too, had been wondering about. "Am I going to be called Andrew Kauffman now, instead of Sandy Collier?"

"No. We've gone by our names for a long time, and I've even had them legally changed. I didn't do it for several years, because I was afraid that court records would just give us away to Daniel Kauffman, if his detectives came across them. Now that he's almost caught up with us anyway, I can't keep changing them. So we are who we are, Sandy."

Megan couldn't stand the suspense any longer. "Are you going to call our other grandfather?"

Her mother hesitated, glanced at Grandpa Davis, and sighed. "I woke up early this morning, thinking about it. Yes, I'll call him, though not from a place where he can trace me. I'm not sure I trust him, no matter what he says. But maybe he's right. He's lost his son, he admits he made some mistakes raising Danny, and he figures you kids are his last chance to do something right. Wasn't that the message, Dad? I hope you aren't mistaken in thinking he couldn't take the kids away from me now that I've proved I can take care of them."

She swiped at the counter with a dishrag, then rinsed it and hung it up. "I think I'd better head on back to . . . well, head on back. I'll call Daniel, but I want to be here when he comes to see the kids, if we agree to do that. Just have a good time here with Grandpa until we get around to it, OK?"

"Mom." Megan sounded husky. "If we aren't going to be hiding any more, can I write to Annie? Tell her what's been happening?"

Mrs. Collier's hesitation was brief. "Sure. Why not? I felt awful about Annie, Megan. Really I did. I hope she understands. You can blame me, and maybe she will."

"Could . . . could I still invite her to come here to the lake, the way we planned? Ben says there's a bus that comes through Lakewood; she could come on the bus."

"If her mother says it's all right. I'll call her, too, when I'm sure about Daniel, as sure as I can be. Now, help me put my stuff in the car, and everybody kiss me goodbye."

It was quiet after her mother had gone. Sandy and Wolf went for a run down the beach, toward the Jamison cabin, so they'd probably come back with Ben, Megan thought.

She didn't follow them, however. She had a different idea in mind.

Grandpa had vanished inside the house. Megan walked quickly at first, slowing to examine the sides of the road before she got to the mailboxes.

How close had the car come last night? Where had it stopped?

It was easy to see. There were tire marks in the soft earth beside the hard-packed roadway, though she couldn't actually make out the tread design.

There was something else that was interesting.

There were footprints.

Megan stared at them—quite clear indentations in a spot of moist earth that was free of grass or twigs.

Someone had gotten out of the car and walked toward the cottage, leaving the car behind.

The others had almost convinced her, earlier this morning, that whoever came in the car was harmless, not interested in the inhabitants of the cottage. Now her pulse quickened as Megan followed the footprints.

It wasn't easy, because they didn't show on the road itself. But occasionally there was a print to one side of the well-traveled area, and after she'd gone about twenty yards, she realized there were two sets.

Both were man-sized. One had smooth soles; the other had waffle treads like those on running shoes.

Two men. The same number as had come in the blue car. What had two men been doing here in the middle of the night, when everyone at the cottage was asleep?

Where Grandpa Davis's driveway turned off the road, she lost the prints entirely because there was grass and patchy dry sand.

She thought about telling Grandpa, then decided he would only think her foolish. It was the detective they had been afraid of, and that matter was taken care of now. After her mother talked to Daniel Kauffman, either they would meet their grandfather, or they would not, but Megan hoped they wouldn't keep running anymore.

Ben and Sandy were putting a couple of boxes into the boat when Megan approached them.

"What's going on? What are you hauling out there now?"

"I'm going to stay overnight again on the island, and Sandy's going until suppertime," Ben said. "We've got so much stuff out there, we might as well use it up. Besides, it's more fun than sleeping in a bed at home. You want to go out for the day, too?"

"I don't know if I should or not," Megan mused. She told them about the mysterious car. "What if they come back? What if they aren't harmless?"

Ben shrugged. "Your grandpa's home, so they won't break in and steal anything. Come on. I brought hamburgers to grill."

"OK," Megan decided. "Are we taking Wolf, or not?"

"Let's not," Ben said. "He takes up too much room."

The big dog had already leaped into the boat. After a brief scuffle, Sandy panted, "Let's let him come, even if it's crowded. I can't get him out unless I throw him overboard, and then he'd probably swim after us."

"It'd serve him right if he drowned," Ben said, but he shoved off and climbed in the boat without insisting Wolf stay behind. Megan thought maybe his tough talk was mostly to cover up what he was really thinking. She was beginning to understand that sometimes, when you hurt a lot, you don't feel like being nice to other people.

They had a good time on the island. They swam off the little cove, cooked their hamburgers at noon, built some more shelves to hold books and the rest of the supplies, and swam again in the afternoon.

While they were drying out on the warm sand, Megan had a sudden thought. "If we take the boat to go home for supper, how are you going to get back to shore, Ben?"

Ben opened his eyes, shading them to look at her. "You mean you aren't going to swim home?"

"No. You're going to have to row us in, then row back."

Ben frowned. "You or Sandy can row home, and then I'll row back. Maybe I'll run home long enough to see if Dad's having anything good for supper, and I'll go back to the island after I've had some of it. He's a lot more mellow since he finished his book. Come on, let's go."

Sandy rowed. Wolf occasionally licked the back of his neck in spite of Megan's attempts to make him sit quietly with her in the bow. The dog didn't wait until they had reached shore before he leaped eagerly overboard, rocking the boat so that Megan, trying to grab him, nearly went over, too.

Water splashed over all three of them when Wolf plunged into the lake, so they were damp and complaining good-humoredly when they nosed into the sandy shore.

It was Megan who came to a halt and interrupted the laughter. "That car is back again. The blue one. I can just see a little of it beyond the trees."

The boys swiveled to look toward the woods. "Let's go check it out," Ben said, and trotted off with Wolf and Sandy eagerly following.

"I'm going to tell Grandpa Davis," Megan said, heading for the cottage.

Her bare feet were soundless on the porch. She had her hand on the screen door when she heard the voice, deep and threatening, inside the kitchen. Megan came to an abrupt halt.

"Oh, you'll tell us, old man. I guarantee, before we're through with you, you'll tell us where those kids are."

Megan froze, sucking in a breath and holding it. All

the fear she thought had faded away after Grandpa Davis talked to that detective came flooding back, worse than ever.

Grandpa's voice sounded strained. "I already told you. Their mother came and got them."

"Yeah? Then why is their junk still here? A pair of tennis shoes drying on the steps, and that Monopoly game out. You playing Monopoly all by yourself?"

"Kids don't always pick things up," Grandpa said, and Megan craned her neck to see inside.

The cold within her grew worse.

Grandpa Davis was sitting on a kitchen chair. The way he held his arms behind him, he must be tied there. There were two men in the room with him, both with their backs to the outside door; Megan was pretty sure they were the same ones she'd seen through the binoculars from the island. They were wearing jeans and plaid shirts. The small, skinny one was dark haired. The taller, more muscular one was blond.

"Go see if there's stuff in the bedrooms, Mac," the dark one said. "Suitcases, clothes, anything like that. I'm betting those kids are still here, or they're coming back." The blond one addressed as Mac headed for the living room, and for a moment Megan's eyes met Grandpa's across the kitchen. She jerked back to the side of the door, chest bursting with the need for air she couldn't seem to draw.

"What are you trying to do, old man? Make me think there's someone behind me, so I'll give you a chance to do something stupid? We're not kidding, mister. We want those kids, and if you get in the way we're not particular if *you* get hurt."

Megan saw the boys emerging from the woods on the

far side of the yard. Ben was grinning. She shook her head violently and waved them back.

For a moment she thought they wouldn't understand her silent message. Then Ben put a hand on Sandy's shoulder, hesitating.

She heard the blond man coming back, heard him say, "They're still here, all right. Their stuff's all over two of the bedrooms."

Megan raised both hands in a pushing motion, and this time Ben definitely understood. He backed away into the shadow of the trees, drawing Sandy with him.

Megan's heart was pounding so that her chest hurt. What should she do? She didn't think she could even get off the porch without the men hearing her or seeing her.

There was the sound inside, a blow, and a muffled cry. "That hurt, old man? You got a broken foot, eh? You want us to break it all over again? Maybe take a hammer to that cast, see how well you do with it off?"

She could hear Grandpa's breathing, harsh, painful. "I told you. My grandchildren went with their mother. Sure, they left things here. They're coming back. But they aren't here now."

Grandpa was trying to protect them from these men, whoever they were. Whatever they wanted.

What could three kids do to save Grandpa from being hurt?

There was a flurry of movement behind her in the kitchen, and then a heavy thudding sound as the chair, and Grandpa Davis, went over onto the floor. Grandpa cried out, and the men yelled at him. Megan, more terrified than she had ever been in her life, ran past the open door and down the length of the porch, vaulting the railing at the end.

She hit hard. Sharp pain went through one ankle, but she kept on running, falling to her knees only when she'd reached the woods. Then she sat down and grabbed the ankle in both hands, rocking back and forth, gritting her teeth.

Ben and Sandy came scrambling toward her, making too much noise in the underbrush, snapping twigs beneath their weight. Wolf licked at her face, and the pain was so severe she couldn't move to push him away.

"What's going on?" Sandy demanded.

Ben was already pulling her hands away from the ankle so he could see it. "Did you break it?"

"I don't know," Megan moaned. "It's starting to swell up already, and it hurts like fury!"

"Maybe it's only sprained. I sprained mine once, jumping off a roof," Ben said. "The doctor said I'd have been better off breaking it; then they could have put a cast on it, like your grandpa's, and I could have walked. I didn't walk on it for nearly a month while the ligaments healed. What's going on in there?"

Megan told them, gasping. The pain was already receding, but she wasn't sure she'd be able to stand on the ankle. "They knocked his chair over, and maybe kicked him. What are we going to do?"

"I let the air out of one of their tires," Ben said. "I thought it would be funny if they tried to drive away and couldn't. Might teach 'em not to hide in the woods and creep up on people. But if they're hurting your grandpa. . . . Maybe I better go get my dad."

"Yes," Megan breathed gratefully. "And hurry!"

Ben was up and running. Sandy looked after him uncertainly. "Shall I go with him, or stay here?"

"Stay here. Help me up. I better see if I can walk," Megan said.

She winced when she put her weight on the sprained ankle. "It's going to hurt, but I can step on it. I will be able to in a few minutes, anyway. Sandy, they're hurting Grandpa! We've got to do something to make them stop!"

Sandy's freckles stood out sharply, and his lips looked white. "What can we do?"

She didn't know the answer to that. "In the movies they create some kind of diversion—you know, make a racket or set a fire or something to draw their attention. . . ."

Sandy glanced around them. "What is there to create a diversion with? We can't start a fire in the woods; it might get out of control and burn up all the cabins and cottages. And what kind of noise could we make that would make them come outside to investigate?"

Megan felt frantic and helpless. "It wouldn't help, anyway, unless we could get Grandpa away before they came back. If we could make *them* go in one direction, while we got Grandpa into the boat, maybe we could get him to the island, only if they saw us . . . Oh, Sandy, I don't know what to do!"

Her brother licked his lips. "Maybe Ben's dad will know."

It seemed hours that they waited for Ben to return, hearing nothing now from inside the cottage. What were the men doing to Grandpa?

# nineteen

THEY HEARD Ben crashing through the brush before they saw him. Megan glanced beyond him, but there was no sign of Mr. Jamison, and her heart sank even before she saw Ben's face.

He threw himself on the ground, chest heaving, so out of breath that he couldn't speak for a few minutes.

"Dad's out on the lake," Ben finally gasped. "Dad *never* fishes, but it looks like that's what he's doing now. He's way over on the other side, I could see him, and I yelled and jumped up and down, but I don't think he knew I was there! I left a note saying we need help, but he probably won't come in time to do us any good. We'll have to think of something ourselves."

Megan's despair must have been written on her face, and her knuckles were white where she clenched her fists.

"Are there any telephones closer than town, to call the police?"

"I don't know. Nobody on the lake has a phone. Dad said that was one reason he liked the cabin. My mom couldn't call him and tell him how rotten I was. He thinks maybe she wants him to take custody of me, because I get on Lawrence's nerves so much. What happened while I was gone?"

"Nothing that we could see or hear. But they said they were going to get the truth out of Grandpa, about where we are. I hope they haven't . . . ," Megan gulped, "killed him."

"That would be pretty stupid. He couldn't tell them anything if he was dead." Ben was getting his wind back, and he crept forward to look toward the cottage. "We've got to create a diversion so they'll come outside, and then we get your grandpa out."

"How?" Megan asked, near tears. "Even if we knew how to drive, Grandpa's car doesn't have the keys in it. They hang on a nail in the kitchen."

"I know how to drive. Well, sort of. I never did it, but I've watched my dad often enough. Look, you work your way around there, Sandy," Ben made a sweeping gesture, "as close to the boat as you can. Be ready to shove off as soon as we draw those guys out of the house far enough so they can't see you. Megan, you go the other way. Sneak up close to the back of the house and stay out of sight. As soon as they're past you, get your grandpa untied and out of there, into the boat."

"How are we going to get them to come out?" Megan asked, testing her weight once more on her sprained ankle. Could she run on it? It didn't seem quite as bad as it had a few minutes ago.

Ben grinned. "I'm going to start their car. Maybe run it into a tree, make enough noise to bring them running. They were stupid enough to leave the keys in it."

"What about you, then? What if you don't have time to get to the boat before we have to shove off?"

"I think I can outrun 'em. I'm a pretty good runner. Besides, I know the woods. *They* don't."

It was a scary plan, and could easily fail if both men didn't investigate the sound of the car, or if they caught Ben or Megan or Sandy, or if Grandpa had been hurt badly enough so he couldn't get to the boat. Still, it was better than not trying to do anything. Megan drew in a deep breath.

"OK. Give us time to get into position before you start the car."

Ben was already gone, crouched over, hurrying. Megan gave Sandy a little push, then took the opposite direction herself, while Wolf trotted after Sandy.

She stayed in the woods as long as she could, then approached the house from the rear. She strained to hear sounds from inside; there were voices, but she couldn't make out the words. Her heart was pounding so hard she was afraid she wouldn't hear the car engine when it started, and she must be ready to run. There wouldn't be a second to spare.

Her ankle was holding up better than she'd thought it might, though she was aware of the deep ache in it. Don't think about it, she told herself. Just think about getting Grandpa away from those men.

The motor of the blue car started up, noisy, harsh. Megan held her breath, and then she heard them coming. Both of them, pounding across the porch and down the steps, cursing.

The gears ground, as if Ben had had trouble finding reverse, and then the motor roared for a few seconds before the impact of metal against tree created a very satisfying crash.

The men ran past Megan's hiding place, which wasn't a hiding place at all, since she was at the end of the porch, in plain sight if they'd turned around.

Then she really did forget her ankle, desperate to reach Grandpa in time.

He was still tied to the chair, but he was humping it across the floor toward the counter where he kept the knives. There was a cut at the corner of his lip, and a bruise was rising below one eye; otherwise, he didn't appear to be hurt.

"Get a knife and cut this rope," he said, and Megan wasted no time in obeying.

"Come on. We've got to get in the boat," Megan said. "Unless you want to get the keys and drive out of here."

"They disabled the car," Grandpa grunted. He pulled his hands free and rubbed them to restore circulation even as he rose so quickly that the chair fell over backward. "Took out the distributor cap. Let's go for the boat."

With him hobbling on his cast, Megan limping on the foot she could suddenly feel again, they ran outside and toward the water.

Sandy was pale and frightened, standing ankle-deep in the water, poised to shove off. Grandpa climbed awkwardly over the bow, nearly falling so that he had to clutch at the sides.

Megan waded out and climbed in over the side, then heard Ben's pelting feet as he dashed out of the woods. He practically hurtled into the boat. "Shove off! Hurry, shove off!"

Wolf was trying to scramble in, too, but he was used to leaping in from shore, not climbing in from the water. He barked and scratched at the rowboat, while Ben fended him off with an oar.

"Not this time, pal," Ben said. "We're too crowded already. Pretend you're a watchdog, and defend us. Come on, Sandy, *let's go!*"

Megan glanced back over her shoulder. "They aren't coming yet. Should we head straight out, where they can't help seeing us when they come back, or go along the shoreline? If we swing in behind the littlest island, and lie low, maybe they won't realize where we've gone."

"Good idea," Grandpa said, and Ben bent his back and pulled strongly on the oars.

"I think I got 'em good," Ben said with satisfaction. "Besides the flat tire, they now have a crumpled fender. Besides that, I threw the keys in the woods."

Grandpa gave a short bark of laughter that sounded more pained than amused. He caught Megan's eyes and said, "They kicked me in the ribs. Didn't break anything, though. They threw my distributor cap into the woods, too. They'll have to find that before *my* car will do them any good."

Ben was pulling hard, too hard, perhaps. He was already tiring. "Let me take a turn," Megan suggested.

"I'll move over, and we'll both row," Ben countered. "Come on, we can both fit on the seat."

Sandy spoke, looking toward shore. "Wolf's trying to swim after us."

"Make him go back," Ben said. "We can't take him in. Do those guys have guns, Mr. Davis?"

"Not that I saw, but I wouldn't put it past them to come up with one," Grandpa said. "Even if they don't, they're strong and they're rough. Certainly I was no match for the two of them. I don't see anybody yet, maybe we've got a chance of pulling this off if that fool dog doesn't give us away." He looked toward Wolf. "Go back! Stay, boy! Stay on shore!"

Poor Wolf paddled after them for a few more yards, then turned and angled for shore, much to Megan's relief. She didn't want him to drown, and they couldn't delay to haul the big dog into the boat, even if there were room for him.

Grandpa twisted around to see the little island where Sandy's American flag still fluttered in the breeze. "Just a few yards farther! This isn't much of an island, but maybe we can hide behind it, unless they walk way down the beach." Megan's arms were aching as badly as her ankle when they stopped rowing and shipped the oars. The exertion had left her damp and exhausted.

The island was barely large enough to conceal the rowboat, and if it hadn't been for the bush, it would have provided no cover for their heads sticking up. Even so, they had to bend over.

"I'm going to crawl up and see what I can see," Ben said after a moment. He was moving his arms experimentally as if he, too, suffered from abused muscles.

The boat drifted, bumping gently against the rock that formed the island. Luckily on this side there was a narrow, flat place Ben could step out onto; Megan reached out to touch the rock with a hand, helping to hold them in position.

"I can't see anything but the cottage," Ben murmured from where he'd stretched out flat and parted the branches with both hands. "Nobody in sight yet."

They couldn't stay here forever, Megan thought, but it was a relief to stop rowing, even for a few minutes. She looked at her grandfather, swallowing hard as she thought of what he'd been through in attempting to protect her and Sandy.

"Who are they, Grandpa? What did they want with us?"

He had taken out a handkerchief and was patting at the corner of his mouth with it. "Names were Guy and Mac, far as I could make out. They didn't introduce themselves." He dipped the handkerchief in the water and patted again. "They didn't explain much, either, but I think I figured it out. They know Daniel Kauffman is your grandfather, and that he was offering a reward for information leading to finding you kids. They're determined to collect it. I told them Daniel's detective had already found you, which seemed to disconcert them a bit. They didn't like that, but they didn't back off. I suspect they're not above kidnapping you and demanding a ransom from Daniel."

Megan shivered. "But how do they know about us? I mean, if they saw us in that TV picture, how did they know who we are, and where we are?"

"Sounded to me like the skinny one—Guy—heard about you from his aunt. Used to be a neighbor to you?"

"Mrs. Morgan!" Megan and Sandy said together.

Megan leaned toward her brother. "Could that be him, Sandy? Mrs. Morgan's nephew, the one who got nasty when your ball went into their yard? I thought you said he had a mustache?"

"He did, but yeah, that could be him. He looks different with his mustache shaved off," Sandy said. "No wonder I didn't recognize him!"

"I never even saw him, just heard Mrs. Morgan talk about him," Megan explained to her grandfather. And then, because she could see that Sandy felt bad about not realizing sooner who the man was, she added, "I don't suppose I'd have known him, either, if he shaved off a mustache."

Grandpa grunted and put the wet handkerchief back in his pocket. "Anyway, this struck him as an easy way to make some money. He hasn't yet thought about how it's probably going to land him in the penitentiary. Or he thinks he's smarter than the FBI, which I doubt. Maybe they found the keys and drove off by now," he added hopefully.

"No. I see them, now. They were in the house," Ben said. "I think they're mad. One of them just kicked that can of rocks off the porch." He hesitated, then went on. "They're coming down to the water. Wolf is jumping around, but he's not biting anybody." He sounded disgusted.

"He's young, and he's only been around a few days. He doesn't know yet who belongs there and who doesn't," Grandpa pointed out. "The thing is, if they figure out we took to the water, they may come after us."

Ben made another report. "No. They must have fixed your car, Mr. Davis. They're getting in it. They're driving away."

They waited then, until it seemed the men were not coming back. At least not immediately. Still, Megan and Ben rowed vigorously when they finally left the shelter of the tiny island and headed for the bigger one, and it was a relief to slide behind it, out of sight from the nearer shore.

Grandpa looked at the steeply sloping rock as they stepped out of the boat. "I couldn't climb into your tree house, so I think I'll just wait for you here," he said. "Looks like a man could get hurt if he slipped on that rock. I'm not part-monkey like the rest of you."

Besides that, Megan saw to her alarm, he was frighteningly pale. She was afraid the men had hurt him more than he had admitted. "Shall we bring you back something to eat?" she asked, offering the only comfort she could think of.

Grandpa inspected the small cove. "That would be nice. I'm not hungry, but it's always a good idea to keep up your strength. We're not safely out of this yet. After the threats they made, and roughing me up, I don't think they're going to want us to get away to the authorities." He eased himself into a sitting position on the sand. "Maybe you could bring me a blanket, too. It'll be cooling off soon."

"Hey," Ben said, "we're not going to spend the night here. After we've rested a few minutes I'll take the boat and go after my dad. If he'd left his keys in the car, I'd have taken it to go for help even if I had to run over those guys to do it. But he must have the keys in his pocket, and he'll get the cops."

Grandpa nodded. "Good. Go before those men come back and see you. They're nasty customers, and we don't know how long they'll be gone. They undoubtedly want to get that car out of there, if it can be traced back to whichever of them owns it."

It was already too late to row across the lake toward Mr. Jamison without being seen, however. By the time Megan had fixed a lunch for her grandfather, and rolled up one of the sleeping bags to take to him, Ben had the binoculars trained on the cottage.

"They're back! Oh, oh! They've figured out where we are, I think!"

Megan took the glasses to scan the shore. The two men were there, all right, with Wolf running up and down the edge of the lake, his antics clearly indicating which direction their prey had taken.

Her lips were so stiff she could hardly speak. "What if

they went to get a gun? Oh, gosh, they're checking out the canoe! They're going to follow us!"

Sure enough, the red canoe was being slid toward the water. Wolf became even more animated, clearly thinking he was to go, too. One of the men kicked at him, but the dog leaped into the canoe before they got it all the way off the beach, then sat down as they'd taught him; Megan could see his tongue lolling happily even from this distance, for the glasses brought him sharply into view.

"I think they're arguing about getting Wolf out," she said, unwilling to relinquish the binoculars. "He doesn't want to get out, and I think they've given up. Yes, they're getting in." She paused, then added, "I don't think they know much about canoes."

"Look up-lake," Ben said. "See if my dad is still out."

Megan swung the glasses, seeing a loon lift from the water in flight, so close she saw water dripping behind it, until she located the yellow canoe that came with the log cabin. "He's just sitting there. Not fishing, just drifting. Resting."

Ben took the binoculars from her hand then, to see for himself. "Yeah. Resting. He always needs to rest when he finishes a book. Hey, I just thought of something. Have you got a mirror with you?"

"A mirror? No, why? Oh, wait a minute. I've got Mom's little bag, and there might be a hand mirror in the pockets. Let me look." Megan scrambled inside to find it.

"Great! The way the sun is, I think maybe I can pick it up in the mirror and signal to him, if he looks this way. I was in a camp once where we learned to signal SOS for help. I forgot everything else, but that one's easy. Three long, three short, three long. Or is it the other way around?

Anyway, it won't matter once I get started. Here, hold these. Watch Dad and see if he reacts to my signals."

Mr. Jamison wasn't asleep, Megan thought thankfully as the glasses brought him nearer. He pushed back his hat and scratched his head, then reached for a can of something, popped the lid off, and drank.

"He's not looking this way," she muttered. "Come on, Mr. Jamison, *please!* Oh, he's looking! Keep signaling, Ben, I think he sees it!"

Ben's father must have seen the tiny blinking flashes. He was shading his eyes now with a hand, staring directly at the island.

"He's coming! He's picked up the paddle, and he's coming!" she squealed.

"So are those guys," Sandy interrupted anxiously. "See? And they're closer than Mr. Jamison. They're going to get here first."

# *twenty*

GRANDPA LIFTED his head to watch them come slipping and sliding down the rocky surface. He looked no better than when they'd left him twenty minutes earlier. He's in shock, Megan thought worriedly.

"Get in the boat, everybody," Ben said. "I'll wait up on top and signal you which way they're coming. We'll take off in the other direction. With a little head start, we'll get out in the open where dad can see us. He saw my signals and he's coming this way," he added by way of explanation to Grandpa Davis.

"What about you?" Megan called after him as Ben turned immediately and went back the way he'd come.

"I'll jump in at the last minute," Ben shouted over his shoulder.

Grandpa got up slowly, as if he were stiff. "Mr. Jamison

is in his canoe? If he'd go for the police—but it's a good hard paddle back to his place."

Megan didn't reply. At least he sounded all right. She joined Sandy in pushing the rowboat partway into the water, concentrating on doing exactly what Ben had said. "Sandy and I will row, so you'd better sit in the back this time, Grandpa. Then Ben can shove off and we'll try to get out of sight before they get here."

It was strange to be speaking that way to a grown-up, but Grandpa just nodded and stepped over the side of the boat, casted foot first to keep it from getting wet.

It didn't work out quite as neatly as Ben had planned, however. The others were ready and waiting when he finally appeared at the top of the slope, but when he turned to look back one last time, his foot slipped. Ben did a somersault on the way down and landed flat on his back, stunned.

For a moment Megan thought he'd been knocked out, for he didn't move. "Ben! Oh, no, we've got to get him into the boat!"

Ben stirred, lifting his head, cradling it in both hands. "Wow! I think I've got a fractured skull, or at least a concussion!"

"Hurry, Ben! Are they almost here?"

"Going around that way." He staggered to his feet and headed toward the others, still holding his head. "They're . . . they're fighting between themselves. I could hear them arguing, and I waited too long. . . ."

He reached the water's edge, but instead of shoving them off, he collapsed on his knees before the bow.

"Get in, hurry!" Megan urged, shipping her oar. She wasn't sure she could drag him in by herself, and there wasn't much maneuvering room for anyone to help her.

Ben let go of his head and made a final effort that landed

him half-in, half-out of the boat, then pushed with the foot that was left on the sand. To Megan's great relief, the boat floated free, and she grabbed for her oar and pulled at the same time Sandy did.

They hadn't taken half a dozen strokes, however, when the red canoe slid into sight around the end of the island. There was still no sign of Mr. Jamison, and she could only hope he hadn't written the mirror signals off as a joke and headed for home without knowing what was going on.

Megan went numb, forgetting the oar, while Sandy pulled harder. The result was that they began to swing around, and then to drift as Sandy, too, ceased rowing.

Ben was bent forward. He lifted his head, and they all stared toward the men in the canoe.

The blond one called Mac held a mean looking club he'd picked up in the woods.

"All right! Back to shore!" he shouted. "Or else I'll have to hurt old Grandpa there some more! Come on, move!"

Wolf, sitting at the far end of the canoe, whined eagerly and quivered with delight to see his friends.

Megan saw the canoe rock a little as Wolf stood up, and the idea came to her, the only idea she had.

"Here, Wolf!" she called out. "Come on, boy, come!"

Wolf didn't hesitate. The canoe rocked violently as he leaped up. For a moment the club was pointed skyward as Mac struggled to keep his balance. Then the big dog went over the side into the water, and the canoe capsized. Mac went backward over the far side; the one called Guy screamed, "I can't swim!" before he followed suit and his head went under.

Wolf was swimming strongly toward the rowboat, but by this time Megan remembered that they'd never been able to haul him into the boat from the water. What did she do now?

Both men had resurfaced, and by this time realized that the rock shelf beneath them made the water shallow. The overturned canoe had drifted beyond the reach of the non-swimmers; they had no choice but to wade to shore. Mac no longer carried the club; it, too, had floated off into deep water.

Ben, still somewhat dazed, gave Megan an admiring grin. "Hey, not bad!" he said. And to Sandy, "Give me a hand, maybe between us we can get him aboard!"

For the following moments, it was touch and go whether Wolf would get into the boat, or the rest of them would be dumped out. And then he was hauled over the side, dripping, shaking, drenching them all, crowded in between everybody's feet. In fact, he was sitting on Megan, but she didn't care.

"Hi, what's going on here?" Mr. Jamison came into view around the far end of the island, taking in the upside-down canoe and the two dripping would-be kidnappers on the little beach.

In the babble of voices trying to explain, with Wolf barking enthusiastically over them all, it was a miracle Mr. Jamison understood any of it. When he did, his mouth was grim.

"I'll get the police. The rest of you follow me to shore. I don't think that pair are going anywhere until the authorities get here."

Megan felt as if her bones had turned to jelly. Her arms were too limp to row any longer, and she was afraid she was going to cry. A few tears did escape, and she hoped if anyone saw them they'd be taken for the water Wolf was still scattering around.

"We'd better rescue your canoe," Ben said. "We can pull it behind us. You want me to row? I'm OK, I think."

Megan pulled herself together. "So am I," she said, and found that she could handle the oar again after all.

From his seat at the back of the boat, Grandpa Davis grinned at her. "You sure are," he said. "All three of you are just great!"

MEGAN SAT at the kitchen table and began to write.

*Dear Annie:*

*So much has happened I hardly know where to begin to tell you about it.*

She paused and chewed thoughtfully on the eraser end of her pencil.

*Maybe I'll just wait until you get here to give you the details. You've probably already heard that Mrs. Morgan's nephew and his friend are in jail for plotting to kidnap Sandy and me and assaulting Grandpa Davis. And next week our new grandfather, that we didn't know we had until a few days ago, is coming to visit us. We feel funny about that. Sandy says he isn't going to like him, because he wasn't very nice to Mom a long time ago. But Grandpa Davis said not to make up our minds until we meet him, because he wouldn't have hired a detective to find us if he didn't care about us. So I'll wait and see.*

She nibbled on the eraser again.

*I'm glad your folks said it was all right for you to visit us. I can't wait to show you my island. We met this boy named Ben, and he helped us build a tree house on it.*

Megan read through what she had written and sign it, *Love, Megan.*

She hesitated, then added a P.S.: *We'll meet you at the bus stop in Lakewood on Thursday.*

"Hey, Megan, come on!" Ben shouted through the screen door. "We're going to explore the islands down at the other end of the lake! You've got an island, and Sandy's got one named for him. Now we're going to see if the last one down can't be King Ben's Island!"

"King Ben!" Megan scoffed. "More like Bossy Ben." She smiled as she wrote one more P.S. on the letter to Annie. *Ben thinks he knows everything, but he does have some good ideas. See you Thursday.*

Then she pushed back her chair and took three apples from the bowl on the table before she went out into the summer sunshine to help Ben stake a claim to his own island.